Of this book, let the critics speak:

'*Unmistakable gold . . .*
All that a book for middle-aged children should be. It will bring a whole chapter of history to life. Altogether a first-class book' – *Catherine King, broadcasting from Perth, Australia*

'The book is about the wool trade of the Cotswolds in 1493. To have made all this an integral part of the story, without any flavour of the history book, is a great feat, and Miss Harnett is to be congratulated. The illustrations greatly enhance the value of a fascinating book' – *Schoolmaster*

'Told simply, with no affected Olde Worlde language . . . about the daily life of a real boy . . . the story is good enough for it to be difficult to put down' – *New Statesman*

'About the medieval wool trade in Cotswold, it is the best children's book I have seen for years. Beautifully illustrated. It holds you in suspense all the time. Unreservedly recommended' – *Western Daily Press*

'Re-creates a Cotswold scene 400 years ago, and is excellently illustrated. The children are charmingly depicted, and the whole atmosphere is attractive. Villainy is unmasked and the good wool merchant saved from ruin' – *Listener*

'Deservedly a prize-winner, a story which children from eleven upwards will find first-rate reading' – *Housewife*

For girls and boys of eleven and upwards

Hal held the horses while Nicholas climbed up to free her (Chapter 9)

The Wool-Pack

WRITTEN AND ILLUSTRATED BY
CYNTHIA HARNETT

PUFFIN BOOKS

Puffin Books, Penguin Books Ltd, Harmondsworth, Middlesex, England
Viking Penguin Inc., 40 West 23rd Street, New York, New York 10010, U.S.A.
Penguin Books Australia Ltd, Ringwood, Victoria, Australia
Penguin Books Canada Ltd, 2801 John Street, Markham, Ontario, Canada L3R 1B4
Penguin Books (N.Z.) Ltd, 182–190 Wairau Road, Auckland 10, New Zealand

—

First published by Methuen & Co. Ltd, 1951
Published in Puffin Books 1961
Reprinted 1963, 1967, 1969, 1971, 1972, 1973, 1974, 1975, 1976,
1978, 1980, 1981, 1984

—

—

Set, printed and bound in Great Britain by
Cox & Wyman Ltd, Reading
Set in Monotype Baskerville

This book gained
the Library Association
CARNEGIE MEDAL
as 'the outstanding
children's book
of 1951'

CONTENTS

NORTHLEACH

At *NORTHLEACH* wool merchants meet and bargain

BURFORD on the Cotswolds is the scene of this story. Nicholas lives at Burford

LEACH'S BARN

At *FARINGDON* the Abbot of Beaulieu has a house

At *NEWBURY* there are many looms for making cloth and a great fair is held there. Cecily lives at Newbury

Pack-horses carry wool across the country

SOUTHAMPTON, a walled city, is a port of many ships, where the galleys land silks and spices and load up with wool-packs

BEAULIEU

BEAULIEU in the New Forest is an Abbey of Cistercian Monks

At *LEPE* the Romans built a Quay

In the ISLE OF WIGHT there is pure drinking water and sometimes a pirate or two

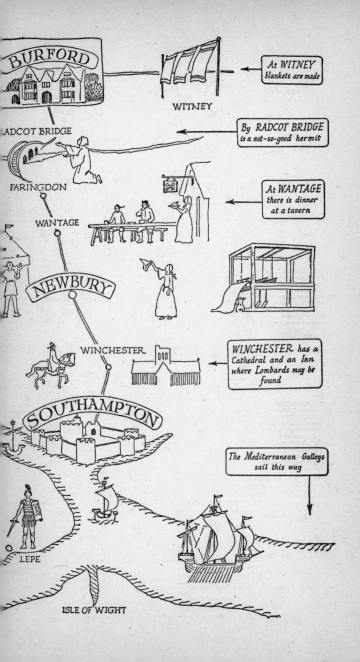

BURFORD

WITNEY

At WITNEY blankets are made

RADCOT BRIDGE

By RADCOT BRIDGE is a not-so-good hermit

FARINGDON

WANTAGE

At WANTAGE there is dinner at a tavern

NEWBURY

WINCHESTER

WINCHESTER has a Cathedral and an Inn where Lombards may be found

SOUTHAMPTON

The Mediterranean Galleys sail this way

LEPE

ISLE OF WIGHT

Nicholas lay on his back on the hill-side

Chapter 1

ALONG THE SKY LINE

NICHOLAS FETTERLOCK lay on his back on the hill-side, gazing up into the young leaves of an oak tree.

He was hot and dirty, and it was good to stretch his full length in the shade. All round him from hills far and near came the bleating of sheep – the high anxious cry of lambs and the deeper reassuring answer of the ewes. Farther away he could hear the voices of the village children. They were wool-gathering down near the river, collecting every fragment of fleece that the sheep had left caught on hedges and bushes. Presently they would take it home to their mothers who would wash it and spin it and make it into warm garments for the winter.

Since early morning Nicholas had been helping with the sheep-washing. It was fun pushing the silly sheep, one by one, off the plank into the river and with long poles making them swim some way down stream before

9

they were allowed to scramble out on to clean pasture. He liked working with the men, Giles the shepherd, and Colin, and Tom, and above all with Hal, the shepherd's son, who was his best friend.

At this moment, however, he was deliberately keeping out of sight. He had played truant from a lesson which he detested. He ought to have washed and dressed and presented himself at the office of his father's factor who taught him all the dull business side of the wool trade. But instead of going, clean and prepared, with his quill pens sharpened, he had just peeped in at the door, all dirty as he was. The factor was not there, so he had slipped away, back to the sheep again.

There would be trouble, too, when he went home. His mother would be angry when she saw him in a herdsman's tunic with bare legs, instead of in his proper doublet and hose. To make matters worse, he smelt; he was quite well aware of it. Sheep were smelly things at the best of times, but wet sheep were the smelliest of all. His clothes fairly reeked, and his mother would be bound to notice it.

It would make no difference to her that the sheep belonged to his father, who was one of the richest wool merchants in the Cotswolds. Did not his father keep a shepherd and endless labourers to do the dirty work? she would inquire. Then with an air of disgust, she would sniff at her perfume ball and send him away to change his clothes.

But, with any luck, the storm would not last. It would all be forgotten tomorrow when his father arrived home from Calais, where he had been attending a meeting of the Staple. The wool trade, England's most important industry, was governed by three hundred leading wool merchants, known as the Fellowship of Merchants of the

Wool Staple, and it was at Calais that they had their headquarters. Nicholas was not sure what happened at these meetings, to which his father journeyed several times a year, but he knew that the Staple fixed all the prices of wool and made endless strict rules which had to be obeyed by everyone who took part in the trade. It was a fine thing to be a merchant of the Staple, and here in the Cotswolds, where everyone made a living out of sheep, his father was counted a very great man. He did not only buy and sell wool grown by other people, as many other wool traders did; but he kept large flocks of his own on the rolling hills. He had built a fine stone house on the outskirts of the little town of Burford, and some day Nicholas would follow in his footsteps and become a merchant of the Staple too.

Lying comfortably in the shade Nicholas was beginning to get drowsy when he was disturbed by the shrill notes of a reed pipe. That was Hal, giving orders to his

Hal giving orders to his dogs

dogs. Nicholas sat up and looked about him. The sheep had moved up the hill, and were now grazing quite near by. Among them, facing the other way, stood Hal, busy with his shepherd's pipe.

Nicholas hallooed through his hands. Hal looked round and started up the slope with his long rolling stride. He was a big lanky fellow, half a head taller than Nicholas, though there was only a month or two between them. His hood was pushed back, and his plain good-tempered face was burned to the colour of copper.

'I didn't know you were here, master,' he called. 'I thought you'd gone to your lesson with Master Leach.'

Nicholas frowned. It gave him a shock when Hal addressed him as 'master'. It was something quite new, evidently an order to Hal from his father the shepherd, and it was a reminder that they were both growing up. From babyhood they had been like brothers, for Hal's mother had been Nicholas's nurse.

'Master Leach was out,' said Nicholas briefly. 'I went to his counting-house, but he wasn't there. I didn't wait long, you can stake your life.'

Master Leach the factor – or wool-packer, as was his proper title – was a cold sour man, and both the boys, in common with everyone else, disliked him heartily.

Hal grinned. 'I saw him by the river an hour since,' he said, 'but he's gone back now. He went towards the town. It's lucky that you did not meet him.'

'I'll stay here,' Nicholas decided. 'He won't be likely to come this way. What are you doing? I heard you signal to the dogs "Go seek, go seek".'

'I'm gathering the ewes,' Hal explained. 'I want to count them all tonight and pen them safely. Then they'll be ready for the washing in the morning. The sooner the washing's done, the sooner the shearing will begin. The shearing supper is going to be a grand one this year.' He smacked his lips, rolled his eyes, and rubbed his middle, to indicate the joys of the feast.

Nicholas laughed. Hal made such comic faces; he

ought to have been a mountebank at a fair. 'Shall I come and help?' he offered.

'Best not,' said Hal. 'Master Leach might spot you. You'd better stay there till he's gone home.'

He whistled to his collies, Fan and Rolf, and went back to the sheep.

*

Nothing loath Nicholas lay down again. He was not a bit repentant about playing truant. All the stuff he was supposed to learn from Master Leach was so dreadfully dull. It consisted mostly of long lists, entered in ledgers, of so many bales of clipped wool, called 'sarplers', and so many sheep skins, called 'wool-fells', to be shipped abroad from London or Sandwich or Southampton, to Calais or to anywhere else abroad that the Staple permitted them to go. He was expected to know all the different grades of wool, their prices, and details of their packing.

These lessons were an extra, for he went every morning to the parson to study reading and writing and Latin grammar. He was willing enough to do that. He liked the parson; there were other boys in his class, and it was a condition of his remaining at home. Otherwise he would have been sent away as an apprentice to London, or else to school at some distant monastery.

He was getting stiff, so he rolled over, and propping his chin on his hands, gazed up the hill.

The old drover's road ran along the ridge from Witney and Oxford in one direction, towards Northleach and far off Gloucester in the other. Against the sky he saw a long line of packhorses pacing eastward, laden with bales of wool. Probably they were from Northleach, five miles away, where the big export merchants

Leach on his piebald

came to meet the local wool-men and bargain for the best of the famous 'fine Cotts'. Packhorses were the only means of carrying the wool, since the river Windrush was not suitable for barges; and this string of patient plodding animals might be going even as far as London.

Close at hand an old man with a stick goaded a reluctant ass up the grassy slope. That was hunchback Hubert from Witney, a familiar figure who came every week to collect the yarn spun by the cottage women and carry it to the weavers to be made into blankets.

Suddenly, from behind a clump of trees a solitary horseman came in sight – a tall figure mounted on a piebald horse. Nicholas caught his breath, and lay very still. The sunlight threw up so vividly the black and white patches on the horse that there could be no mistake. It was Master Simon Leach the wool-packer. Evidently he had given up any idea of Nicholas's lesson, locked his counting-house, and was going back to his home at Westwell a couple of miles away. Nicholas watched him as he crossed the road at the top of the hill and vanished down the other side. Then he gave a sigh of relief. As he had often been before, he was thankful for that piebald horse, so easily recognized from a distance. Now he could go home.

But as he sat up and stretched himself a distant gleam of light caught his eye. A little party of horsemen was approaching from the east. They were too far off for him to see what they were, but the glint could only come from the reflection of the sun on armour. There seemed to be about six of them, though only the last four were men-at-arms. Now who could be riding with an armed escort in these days? A few years ago, before the Wars of the Roses were ended, it would have been quite common to see soldiers in armour. But it was nearly eight years since the battle of Bosworth Field, where King Richard the Third had been killed, and King Henry Tudor had put on the crown, and nowadays everything was peaceful.

By this time the little procession was near enough to be seen clearly. In front rode two fine gentlemen, one tall and elegant on a big grey horse, the other small, dressed in black and slouched in the saddle. Behind them came four guards with steel caps and cuirasses, leading a laden baggage horse.

Nicholas decided that they were merchants, and wealthy ones, too. He noticed that a dog, a tall gazehound, trotted on leash beside the grey horse. They must certainly be people of importance to travel with such an array. He wondered for a moment who they were and where they were going.

A little party of horsemen

All at once, without a second's warning, chaos broke loose. The merchants' horses, which had been so quiet and well-behaved, suddenly reared. There was a stamping of hoofs, a jangle of harness, and sharp cries in a foreign tongue. Nicholas could not make out what had happened until he saw a small dark shadow come streaking like an arrow down the hill towards him. It was a hare, and after it, coursing with all the power of its supple body, came the merchant's gazehound.

Nicholas jumped to his feet, startling the hare. It doubled back, darted down the field and headed straight into the midst of the grazing flock, with the hound close behind it. Sheep stampeded in every direction. The hound lost sight of its quarry. It hesitated, and in the twinkling of an eye the collies were upon it, and all three dogs rolled over and over, biting and snarling in a savage fight.

Nicholas started to run towards them, but dodged just in time as, with a thunder of hoofs, the small man in black galloped by. Hal had rushed upon the scene, crook in hand, and now the horseman swept down upon them all, laying about him with his riding-whip. He lashed out savagely, raining blows indiscriminately, as much upon Hal as upon the dogs. Nicholas tore along the field shouting just as Hal darted out of range with the blood streaming down his face.

But the whip had done its work. The sheepdogs drew off and the gazehound freed itself; and, in obedience to the shrill note of a whistle, speeded back towards the top of the hill. Nicholas made a grab at Fan, who was yelping from the lash, while Rolf, starting after the hound but hopelessly outpaced, lay down panting.

The man on horseback trotted round in a circle and came back. His face was sallow and pock-marked, with little eyes that peered under heavy lids, and a large flabby mouth. A black fur-edged gown hung from his high shoulders, and he wore a wide black hat with a long feather.

He halted beside the boys, and looked from one to the other.

'Maybe your cur-dogs have learned a lesson,' he said in a clipped foreign voice. 'Whose sheep are these that you are minding?'

Nicholas had gone white with anger. 'They are my father's sheep,' he replied boldly, 'and my father is Master Thomas Fetterlock, of the Fellowship of the Staple, at your mastership's pleasure. Your dog attacked his sheep, and you have beaten his servant. He shall hear of it when he returns.'

Clearly the stranger was astonished. He looked the boy slowly up and down from head to foot, while Nicholas became more and more acutely aware that his face was dirty and his legs were bare. Then with an unpleasant leering smile, the man swept off his hat in a bow so exaggerated that Nicholas knew that it was done in mockery.

'I ask your pardon that I did not recognize your father's son,' he said pointedly. 'The hound did but course a hare. It is unfortunate that he should have disturbed the sheep. But as it happens our meeting is apt. Let me present myself. On the hill yonder you see my lord, Messer Antonio Bari of Florence, agent of the noble banking house of the Medici. I am his humble secretary. We are on our way to your worshipful father's house, to sup with him.'

Once again he bowed low, as though to someone of importance, and Nicholas, red to the roots of his hair, returned the bow with as much dignity as he could

'Maybe your cur-dogs have learned a lesson'

muster. He explained that his father was away on business of the Staple and was not expected home before the morrow.

The secretary smiled again.

'You are behind the times, young sir,' he said. 'Your father is but a few miles off. We met him in Oxford and were honoured with an invitation to sup and sleep at his house in Burford. A messenger has ridden ahead to tell your lady mother.'

Nicholas bowed again with tight shut lips. It was all news to him. He had never heard his father speak of these foreigners. If they were bankers he supposed that they must be Lombards. All bankers seemed to be Lombards.

The secretary, on the point of riding away, hesitated and came back.

'Could you of your goodness direct me to the house of one Master Simon Leach in this neighbourhood?' he asked.

That was easy. Glad to be able to assert himself Nicholas said promptly that Master Leach was his father's packer, that he lived at Westwell, and had just gone home – only a short while ago. He turned to point out the direction when he noticed that the Lombard looked strangely taken aback.

'Your father's packer?' he repeated quickly. 'I did not know. I thank you for your courtesy, young sir.'

He wheeled his horse and with a polite reminder that they would meet again later, he rode swiftly away.

For one moment Nicholas watched him, wondering what had made him break off so abruptly, and what on earth a Lombard banker could want with Leach the packer.

Then he turned to look for Hal.

The shepherd's home

Chapter 2

SHEPHERD'S COT

HAL had gone down to the river to swill water over his head. Nicholas met him coming up again, wiping two ugly red weals tenderly with his old woollen hood.

Nicholas's wrath was bubbling over. 'The cowardly knave,' he cried. 'Are you much hurt? I'd like to see the colour of his blood.'

'He had a face like a toad,' said Hal contemptuously. 'But his plaguey dog scattered the sheep. We must get them in quickly or they will be half across the parish. Do you take Fan and go up the hill, and I will go down with Rolf.'

In their fright the sheep had indeed strayed far and wide. Hal's reed pipe was kept busy guiding the dogs. 'Go seek, go seek.' 'Hold! Hold!' 'Fetch them in, fetch them in.' Fan and Rolf knew the notes as well as Nicholas did. They guided the flock into the fold through a gap in the stone wall, and Hal counted as the sheep passed in, using his father's own special tally rhyme.

Eggum, peggum, penny leggum
Popsolorum Jig:
Eeny, meeny, ficcaty fee
Dil dol domini
Alla beranti, middle di danti,
Ficcaty forni a rusticus.

Nicholas murmured the words under his breath. He had known them from babyhood, though he had no idea what they meant. He'd first learned them from Meg, Hal's mother, when she was his nurse, and they reminded him of the warm stuffy smell of wood smoke, wet wool, and mutton stew in Meg's cottage.

When Hal was satisfied that none of the sheep were missing they closed the gap in the fold with hurdles. Nicholas glanced at the position of the sun. The shadows had not yet begun to lengthen. Supper would not be ready for a couple of hours.

'I'll come home with you,' he announced to Hal. 'I'd just like to see your father's face when you tell him what happened. And he may know why that ugly master should ask the way to Leach's house.'

Hal had not heard the secretary inquire for Leach. He was quite excited about it, and certain that his father would be interested. There was little love lost between the shepherd and the packer. Giles was an old servant, who had started work under Nicholas's grandfather, while Simon Leach was comparatively a newcomer whom Master Fetterlock had brought from London. Leach was trained in all the latest business methods and stood high in his employer's favour. But the master was often away on the business of the Staple in Calais and knew too little of what went on among his Cotswold flocks. Old Giles often shook his head about it, and Nicholas knew that he not only disliked the packer but distrusted him.

The two boys, with the dogs, left the bare hill-side, and turned towards the valley where the silvery Windrush curved among the willows, and where the shepherd's cot lay on a sheltered slope. It was a cosy little house of plastered timber and thatch, set about with barns and pigsties, dovecot and beehives and fenced garden patch.

Nicholas had been reared there with Hal as his foster brother. There had been only one room in those days, a room without a chimney where the smoke billowed round and round before it found its way out of a trap-door in the roof. Since then it had been improved by the addition of a big stone chimney built up through the middle of the cottage, so massive that it supported the beams for the floor of a tiny bed-chamber in the angle of the thatched roof. Nicholas remembered how he and Hal as children had delighted in creeping up and down the ladder stair for the excitement of the climb. Hal slept in that little room now, and Nicholas still envied him.

Inside the shepherd's cot

All the happiest memories of his childhood were centred in this tiny cottage. At home he had continually to remember his manners. He might never sit in the presence of his parents without their leave, nor raise his voice, nor speak unless spoken to. His father was indulgent and seldom beat him – far too indulgent his mother said, when in some moment of extreme exasperation she so far forgot her duty as to criticize her husband. But there was no freedom for Nicholas at home as there was here under the shepherd's roof, where he could behave as any ordinary healthy boy, and where, into the bargain, he enjoyed the privileges of being 'the young master'.

On this spring afternoon, smoke was rising from the stone chimney and the shutters were down, leaving the window spaces open in both walls – a sure sign of warm still weather, since if it were cold or stormy only the side away from the wind could be open. A trestle table and a couple of benches stood outside the cottage and through the window space Meg, a plump homely little woman in a shapeless woollen gown, was setting on the table spoons made of sheeps' bone, some wooden bowls, and a pitcher of baked clay.

When she saw the boys she came to the door.

'There has been a message for you, young master,' she called to Nicholas. 'Your lady mother sent to look for you because there is to be company to sup.' Then she caught sight of Hal, and forgot Nicholas. 'God save us, boy, look at your head. What have you been at?'

While she mixed a poultice of bread and sour milk and slapped it on her son's brow, he and Nicholas told of the dog fight and the scattered sheep. She listened with little clucking noises of anger and dismay.

'A plague on all foreign knaves,' she cried. 'I wish the

The shepherd's tools

dogs had gone for him instead of for his hound. A shame that you must sup with him at your father's table, Master Nicholas. I've been making some of your favourite little cakes on the griddle too, and now, with a feast to come, you'll not be able to eat them.'

Promising cheerfully that no feast could spoil his appetite for her cakes, Nicholas followed her indoors. A table, fashioned roughly from a tree trunk, held the remains of Meg's cooking, a big bed was built into the wall, and on pegs by the door hung the shepherd's cloak, the tar-box and searing iron with which he doctored his flock, his lantern and spare crook. It was all warmly familiar, and Nicholas stooped to pet one of the delicate lambs that lay bedded on hay in a corner.

Over the fire, a griddle swung from a hook. Meg swept two or three hot crisp little cakes from it into the boys' out-stretched hands, and stood laughing to watch the old game of 'Catching the devil with hot tongs' as they tossed them about till they were cool enough for their teeth to tackle. Then burned tongues had to be soothed with draughts of ewe's milk, and once more the sense of home possessed Nicholas. In his mother's house they drank only cow's milk.

He was still draining the mug when a joyful clamour from Fan and Rolf announced that their master, Giles, had come home. He had been, Meg said, to help her brother the barber-chirugeon at his shop in the town. It was part of a barber's business to extract teeth, set broken limbs, and perform any small operation needed by the townsfolk. Sometimes when the case was a difficult one, or the patient full of fight, Nash, the barber, appealed to his brother-in-law. Like most shepherds Giles had learned wisdom in the folds, and an ailing human was not, in his eyes, very different from an ailing sheep. He was also a strong man, and accustomed to holding down struggling ewes.

As Nicholas heard the shepherd's voice, he set down his mug, dropped a hasty kiss on Meg's apple cheek, and went outside.

Hal now wore a bandage so, of course, his father inquired what was the matter, and once more they told their story.

Giles, a tall old man with a furrowed face and shaggy grizzled hair, sat down on the bench by the window, then, with a side glance towards 'the young master', half got up again till Nicholas also seated himself.

At first the boys' tale amused him, but gradually the smile faded from his face, and when Nicholas came to the part about Leach, he thumped the table with his fist.

'The Lombards!' he cried. 'Leach in the hands of the Lombards? By Heaven, I might have guessed it.'

Nicholas looked at him blankly. He had expected Giles to enjoy a bit of gossip, but he had not anticipated a storm.

'What do the Lombards do?' he asked doubtfully. 'I'm always hearing people talk of Lombards, and everyone seems to hate them, but, to tell the truth, I don't understand why. They are foreigners from North Italy, that much I know. His mastership out on the hill said that they were bankers.'

At first the boys' tale amused him

'*Bankers?*' snorted Giles. 'That's too sweet a name for it, master. *Usurers* would be better; and Holy Church condemns all usury. They ride round the country lending money at vast interest to any who are in difficulties — that is if they have something to offer in pledge. People say they have half the traders of England in their power. They buy wool too, direct from the growers, and ship it abroad as they will, which is more than an Englishman may do. The Staple itself cannot stop them because they hold their licences direct from the King. 'Tis said that even he is in their debt and dare refuse them nothing.'

Nicholas frowned. He was still not sure what all these words meant – 'usury' and 'interest' – though he saw plainly enough that it had something to do with borrowing money and having to pay back more than you borrowed. But if these Lombards were as bad as all that, would his father have invited them to sup? He said this to Giles.

The old shepherd shook his head.

'Your father is a great merchant, sir. Doubtless he knows what he is about. And I've heard that some of the Lombard bankers are fine lords.' He turned on Nicholas a pair of keen blue eyes. 'But all the same, Master Nicholas, I'd like to know what they want with Simon Leach.'

There was a pause while Meg filled her husband's bowl with steaming mutton broth. He crossed himself, broke off a hunk of barley bread, dipped it and sucked it thoughtfully.

'Have you seen Leach's new barn, young master? He has built for himself a big stone barn, right out on the wolds. Now Leach is a member of the Guild of Wool-packers, and by law wool-packers are not allowed to trade in wool for themselves. Would you tell me, then, what he wants with a great new barn?'

This certainly was a poser. Nicholas said he thought that Leach had some sheep of his own.

'He may have a dozen ewes for his own needs,' Giles

admitted testily, 'but no man builds a barn like that for a dozen ewes. It is always locked. What does he keep inside it? No, Master Nicholas, say what you will, there are things afoot in these parts that I like not. The old labourers are gone. It is Leach's business to find others. He is engaging strange men from distant parts. Some of them scarce know one end of a sheep from the other.'

'Have you told this to my father?' inquired Nicholas.

The shepherd shook his head. 'You well know, sir, that your worshipful father is not an easy man. He is just and true in every word, and a kind master, but he does not like to take advice. The man Leach has won his favour and he will not hearken to me. All the same as soon as the shearing is safely past I will seek to speak with him again.'

At mention of the shearing both boys cheered up. The sheep shearing was the great event of the Cotswold year. All the local wool-dealers, as well as the agents of the big Staple merchants, came riding round the farms taking samples of the wool and bidding for the proceeds of the clip. Sometimes a fleece was sold even before it left the sheep's back. And when it was all over there was the shearing supper given by every master for his men, with lots to eat and drink, and singing and dancing far into the night.

Last year was the first time that Nicholas had been allowed to remain at the supper with the men, instead of going home early with the women and children, and he, as well as Hal, was looking forward eagerly to this year's feast. He began to question Giles. When would the clip begin? How long would it last?

But before the shepherd could answer, the sound of a distant bell came floating along the valley. It was the clock from the tower of Burford Church striking the hour of five. Nicholas started to his feet, remembering that the Lombards were coming to supper, and, what was more, that his father would be home. He must change his clothes, and if he did not hurry, he would be late.

Fetterlock House

Chapter 3

THE LOMBARDS

HE set off at a brisk trot across the fields. The little town of Burford in the valley ahead of him lay bathed in a mellow golden light. Even the faces of the new stone houses, so hard and so clean, were softened till they toned with the timber and thatch of the old ones. There had been a wave of building in the last few years. Now that the Wars of the Roses were really over and there was a King who cared for peace, it was worth while to spend some of the money earned in the wool trade. A couple of jingling lines came into Nicholas's head as his feet jogged along:

> I thank God and ever shall
> It is the sheepe hath payed for all.

Those words were graved on the glass window of a house which another merchant of the Staple had built near Newark. His father quoted them so often that Nicholas wondered why he didn't put some such lines on his own new house, though he supposed that his mother would not have been pleased. She hated sheep and liked to imagine that she was a lady of rank married to a gentleman of coat armour, instead of the daughter of a Bristol shipowner wed to a wool trader with a merchant's mark.

Nicholas left the fields just where the muddy road ended, and the cobbles of Witney Street began. The fine spring evening had brought all the women to the doors of their cottages, each with a distaff tucked under her arm, busily dropping, twisting, and winding up a spindle as she gossiped. Some of the well-to-do possessed new-fangled spinning wheels; but spinning wheels were heavy cumbersome things, and, wheel or no wheel, every good wife carried the old-fashioned distaff and spindle with her always. There were odd moments all through the day when she had at least one hand free, and every spool of spun yarn was of value. Nicholas would not for worlds have admitted it, but he loved a spindle. Meg had taught him to use one when he was young. He liked dropping it on the end of a length of rough wool drawn from the distaff, and watching it twiddle round and round, winding the wool into a firm thread. It was fun catching it again at the exact moment before it began to untwist, just as much fun as whipping a peg top in the market-place, but because it was woman's work, he never dared to confess that he liked it.

He bade a civil 'God keep you' to the women who smiled at him, and trotted across the broad High Street which swept down-hill to the Church with its new stone steeple. The Fetterlock house was in Sheep Street on the outskirts of the town, facing over the roof tops and across the valley. The entry was by a wide stone passage through the house to a courtyard beyond. Nicholas dodged round to the side, hoping to slip in unnoticed by the buttery door. But he was unlucky. As he tiptoed across the courtyard his mother emerged from the passageway.

He sighed. He had known that it would happen. Nothing escaped his mother's sharp eye, nor her delicately-pointed nose.

He saw at a glance that she was dressed for a grand occasion. She wore her best gown of violet cloth, edged all round the skirt with marten fur and the kirtle worn under it, which showed at neck and hem, had a thread of gold in it.

In spite of all this finery she still carried under her arm her little dog, Bel – a spoilt sharp-nosed little creature which went everywhere with her. Nicholas loved dogs, but Bel, who could not play a game without whimpering or snapping, was more than he could stand. His father hated Bel too, but every gentlewoman carried a tiny dog, so, of course, Mistress Fetterlock could not be denied.

She stared at her son, sniffed, raised her brows, and told him crisply to go and change his clothes. He stank of the sheep fold. Nicholas wanted to laugh. It was so exactly as he had pictured it. But he said nothing, even when she told him that his father was coming, and that there were guests. He almost asked about the Lombards, who they were, and where they came from, but he checked himself. Probably his mother would not know. His father told her little of his business matters. So he answered only 'Yes madam', obediently.

He was half-way up the stairs when she called him

back and told him to go and wash at the well trough. He mastered his impatience once more, and caught up a towel which hung behind the buttery door. His mother had a mania for washing, not only hands and face, but washing all over. Once a week the women servants were packed off to bed early and a large tub was set down in front of the kitchen fire. His father got into it first, and Nicholas second, with fresh hot water added from the cauldron. Very often the men servants were told to follow on, and the scullion boy last, before he had to mop up the mess. Of course everyone had foot-baths, particularly after a journey, and Nicholas loved a dip in the river. But a tub every week was really carrying it a bit far.

However the water was refreshing enough, and Nicholas held his bare legs in it. Then he rubbed himself dry, and made another attempt to get upstairs unnoticed. This time he was successful.

He slept in a room at the top of the house, and unless there were many guests he had it to himself. His mother had made it gay with hangings of a blue and yellow striped cloth called Ray. There was glass in the windows, and one casement was made to open. It was all very novel in 1493.

Nicholas shook himself out of his comfortable tunic, and opened the chest which stood at the foot of the bed to find his best clothes. The hose lay just on the top. They were made of cloth cut on the cross, so that they fitted his legs neatly. They were tied by laces called 'points' to his overshirt or pourpoint – a little short jerkin worn for the sole purpose of holding up the hose. He tied the points with great care, remembering an occasion when he had dressed in a hurry and his hose had descended while he was waiting at table. There had

He tied his points with great care

been guests then too – another Staple merchant, Master Midwinter from Northleach, a fat jolly man, who had never seen Nicholas since without inquiring if he was sure of his points.

Hose once on, he knelt in front of the chest and rummaged for the rest of his things. He pulled out a doublet of russet cloth with a row of silver buttons down the front, a pair of shoes in soft scarlet leather, fringed with leather loops – he really loved those shoes – and finally a 'cote' of dark red Camlet with loose hanging sleeves. It would hide the fact that his doublet was too small. He had outgrown most of his clothes, and a new outfit was being made for him. Never before had there been such a fuss about it. A tailor even came all the way from Oxford to measure him.

He was combing his hair in front of a small mirror of polished steel when he heard the clatter of horses in the road below. Cautiously he peeped down.

The two Lombards were in the act of dismounting, their bridles held by a couple of his father's men. He recognized the little round-backed secretary in black and looked past him to the bigger man, Messer Antonio Bari, the agent of the Medici.

By comparison Messer Bari was immensely tall. His hair was long, resting on his shoulders. He had a large aquiline nose, and he wore with an air of distinction a magnificent gown of crimson brocade turned back to show a rich fur lining. As he strode up the short path to the house, Master Thomas Fetterlock stepped out to meet him.

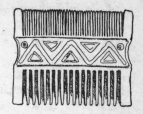

Nicholas's comb

Nicholas could see only the top of his father's head, but he dodged back and scrambled into his doublet. He had not realized that his father had arrived. He finished his toilet quickly, pushed his old clothes into the chest and tiptoed out on to the landing. As all seemed quiet below he crept downstairs.

But careful as he was, once more his mother heard him. She called him into the hall.

Seeing him so spruce and clean her face relaxed and she smiled at him. He took in two things at a glance. The first was that the hall had been cleaned out. The soot and cobwebs from the winter's fires and candles were gone, the stone hearth was clear and empty, and there were new rushes on the floor, crisp and springy to the tread. The second thing was that supper was laid in the hall instead of, as usual, in the dining parlour. A white damask cloth covered the long refectory table, and every piece of silver and glass that the household could muster was laid out – jugs and flagons, goblets and cups, a knife-stand with knives enough for everyone, a silver trencher for each place, and in the centre a great Salt, made in the shape of a galley of wrought silver. It was clear that these guests were important ones.

Even before his mother opened her mouth, Nicholas knew just what she was going to say. He was to carve. This was all an old grievance. If his mother had got her way, he would have been sent for his education to the

house of a nobleman to serve as a page and learn the
ways of polite society. But his father would have none of
it. The boy was to be a merchant, he said. Not to be
denied, his mother had herself educated him in what she
called 'civilized ways'. She taught him to carve, to wait
at table, to sing, to fetch and carry – all the things he
would have learned as a page. And on the rare occa-
sions when there was company at home, she expected
him to do her credit.

'Of course,' she was saying now, 'you will carve the
meats. Or would you rather have charge of the wine?
Bernard doesn't really carve badly, though he is only a
pantryman.'

Nicholas said quickly that he would carve. To pour
wine with all those fine clothes about would be too
great an ordeal.

'Very well,' his mother agreed. 'There are two fat
ducks and a couple of capons, a boar's head, a venison
pasty, and the usual roasts; carve them skilfully as you
well know how. And whatever you do, put no gravy on
your father's platter; he hates to get his fingers greasy.
I do not suppose that the foreigners will care. When
you've served everyone, you can take your own platter
and sit on the stool at the end of the table. And mark, the
knives are very sharp. Hold the birds firmly by the legs
as I have shown you and be careful.'

'Yes, madam,' said Nicholas meekly. He knew of old
that it was safest to agree to everything, as a good son
should, so he bowed. Then he tried to edge towards the
door, but again she called him back.

'Do not forget the handwashing,' she reminded him,
'both before the meal begins, and after it. Take the
silver ewer and bowl to your father and the guests, pour
a little water over their fingers and offer the napkin.'

Then, as Nicholas could not resist a sigh, she told him not to look stupid. In church he had served Mass often enough, and this was just the same as the Lavabo, where he poured water over the priest's fingers.

To change the subject he inquired where his father was.

'In the garden with his guests,' Mistress Fetterlock replied. 'You had better go out and be presented before supper. But mind that you are ready for your duties when I call you.'

*

The garden, at the back of the house, was shady with fruit trees, and the fallen apple blossom lay like pink snow on the tops of clipped box hedges.

The three men were pacing up and down a long grass alley, newly scythed, Master Fetterlock and the little secretary deep in discussion, while Messer Antonio Bari listened with a faint air of amusement, and twiddled under his nose a stem of lily of the valley.

Nicholas waited for them to turn. He considered whether he must kneel and ask his father's blessing. It was usual when his father had been away. And yet, somehow, he was loath to drop on his knees before that ill-favoured little foreigner.

While he hesitated his father looked round. His tired face brightened as he saw Nicholas, and without waiting for any greeting, he laid an arm across the boy's shoulder and drew him to his side.

'This is my son,' he said simply. And Nicholas, warming at the note of pride in his father's voice, made a deep obeisance to his father's guests.

The tall Lombard smiled as he acknowledged the salute, but the secretary looked Nicholas up and down with the same offensive stare as before.

Nicholas made a deep obeisance

'I met your young mastership on the field, I think,'
he said. 'Or have you maybe a brother? I should not
have known you. Your air is vastly different.'

Nicholas turned crimson. Hal was right; the man had

a face like a toad! Of course his air was different. Did the blockhead expect him to sup in a herdsman's tunic, or to tend sheep in a good gown? But he stifled his wrath and inquired politely if their worships had safely found the way to Westwell.

Immediately there was some confusion. Both the Lombards answered at the same time. The secretary said something about missing their road to Burford, and Master Antonio tapped Nicholas lightly on the shoulder.

'Can you name me some of these flowers, young sir?' he begged. 'They grow also in Italian gardens, but I do not know their English names.' He leaned towards Nicholas confidentially. 'They are talking money,' he whispered, jerking his head over his shoulder. 'I don't know how you find it, but for myself I detest figures. When I was your age I could not add two and two.'

The thought entered Nicholas's head that it was strange for a banker to hate figures. But Messer Antonio's smile was so friendly that he put the idea aside. After all, even Giles had admitted that there were honest men among the Lombards.

Messer Antonio was deeply interested in the garden. He would like to beg roots of some of these flowers, he said, to take back to his home near Florence. He described his house on a sunny hill-side, next to the lovely villa of his beloved master, Messer Lorenzo de Medici, called the Magnificent, who died, alas! a year ago. Over his heart he made a little sign of the cross and murmured '*requiescat in pace*', which Nicholas politely repeated after him. Doubtless, he said, his young mastership would have heard of Lorenzo Il Magnifico – the greatest man of the age. He drew from his pouch a large bronze medal, modelled in relief, showing the

A portrait in bronze

profile of a plain man with a crooked nose.

Nicholas held it in his hand. 'It is very heavy,' he remarked. 'Is it a coin?'

The Lombard shook his head.

'It is a portrait of Il Magnifico,' he said. 'Read the inscription round the edge. "Magnus Laurentius Medices." We have a fashion for such things in Italy. The artist models the original from life; then a mould is made from it, and one can have as many copies cast as one wishes. In that way one can give one's portrait to all one's friends. A very good idea, you will agree.'

Nicholas said 'Yes' as he turned the medal round. He was wishing secretly that his father would have a portrait done that way.

'Is it a good likeness?' he inquired.

'A speaking likeness,' sighed Messer Antonio. 'We were boys together. I loved him dearly – and his brother Giuliano too. Giuliano was my own age. We had the same foster-mother.'

Nicholas nodded sympathetically. That was like himself and Hal. He inquired if Messer Giuliano was in Italy?

'Alas, he is dead too,' said the Lombard sadly. 'He was killed in the Pazzi Conspiracy – but you will not know about that. It all happened fifteen years ago – surely before you were born. Messer Giuliano was stabbed to death in the Cathedral at Florence. I was there.'

Nicholas gasped. This sounded like a thrilling story.

'Did your mastership see it?' he asked breathlessly. 'Was it in war that it happened?'

'There was no war. It was a base and cowardly plot,' said Messer Antonio grimly. 'The Medici were virtually the rulers of Florence. But there were others who were mad with jealously, and wanted to seize the power for themselves. They planned to poison the two Medici brothers, Lorenzo il Magnifico, and my beloved Giuliano. When that fell through they sought to stab them at a feast in Lorenzo's house. But that failed too. So, to crown their wickedness, they chose the most solemn moment of the High Mass in the cathedral. As all our heads were bowed in prayer the murderers struck.' He gave a shudder. 'I shall never forget it.'

'Did they stab them both?' cried Nicholas. 'Did they get Il Magnifico too?'

Messer Antonio shook his head. 'God be praised, Il Magnifico escaped with only a wound. The hand of the villain who struck him trembled – as well it might at such a moment. But Giuliano fell dead. The people of Florence, who adored the Medici, seized the men who were responsible and hanged them on the spot from the top of the Palazzo della Signoria, that is – how would you call it in English? – the Palace of the Government. The Archbishop of Pisa was mixed up in it, and they hanged him also. It was a terrible day.'

Nicholas was eager for more. 'What happened next?' he demanded.

Messer Antonio smiled at his excitement. He slipped a hand through the boy's arm and they, too, strolled up and down the shady garden.

But they had not got much further with the story when from the house came Mistress Fetterlock to call them to supper. Her furred gown was lifted to display the embroidered kirtle, and her crisp coif was stirred by the evening air. At a nod from her, Nicholas sped to fetch his ewer and basin; but his head was full of conspiracies and stabbings, and he scarcely noticed over his shoulder the polite scene of bowings and courtesies that was going on behind him.

He ate greedily, cramming his mouth

Chapter 4

THE SUPPER PARTY

THE long table with its white cloth was elegantly arranged. The great silver Salt stood in the middle, and before each place was a folded napkin, a silver platter, a knife, a spoon, and a manchet – that is a large roll of wheaten bread with which to mop up gravy. Farther down the room a court cupboard displayed more silver and a fine array of flagons of wine. There were three chairs, for his father, his mother, and their principal guest. The secretary and himself would sit on stools, but each had a velvet cushion embroidered by his mother's own hand. It was very grand and Nicholas felt a sudden wave of pride. These Lombards, bragging away about their Italian lords, would see that a Merchant of the Staple was a great man too.

In the pantry he tied an apron over his fine clothes and set about this very particular business of severing the joints of the ducks and the capons. Bernard, the pantler, a slow-witted yokel, whom Mistress Fetterlock delighted to refer to as her 'steward', helped him to arrange them on large pewter dishes, trussing them back into the shape of birds again with skewers. Nicholas

43

would rather have had Dickon, his father's man, to help him. Dickon was a cheerful little cockney, half clerk, half body-servant, who went everywhere with the Master. But Mistress Fetterlock did not approve of Dickon, and kept him in the background. Tonight, however, Nicholas boldly directed him to serve the wine. Dickon could be trusted not to spill it. His mother might not be pleased, but after all, thought Nicholas, as he wiped the grease from his hands, if he was made to carve, he had the right to arrange matters in his own way.

He was just taking off his apron when the sound of voices in the passage warned him that the company was approaching. He seized the silver ewer and bowl, laid the napkin across his arm and had just time to spring to position beside the table as they came into the hall.

When they were all in their places, his father said a short Latin grace – he was punctilious in such matters. Then Nicholas, beginning with the guests, took his basin to each in turn.

Messer Antonio, looking round him, remarked politely that it was a beautiful room. It was not often that one saw such fine workmanship in a small town; but this was a neighbourhood of good stone and the chimney piece no doubt had been carved by a local mason. At the oak wainscot, fitted in panels from floor to ceiling, he gazed with fixed attention. Surely no country joiner had wrought that pattern resembling folded linen; it looked like the work of a master craftsman from London or Oxford.

Nicholas took his attention from his serving to follow the Lombard's eyes. It had never dawned on him before to think the room beautiful. It was long, with a window built out in front and filled with many small panes of glass. The wainscot, which their guest admired so much, was a pale honey colour and threw a warm reflected light from the beams of the setting sun. At either side of the stone fireplace a fine Arras tapestry was hung against the wall. His father had brought them home strapped to the back of his saddle after one of his journeys to the continent.

'Boy,' hissed Mistress Fetterlock as Nicholas stared round a moment too long. Jerked back to earth by a sharp slap on his ear, he set down the ewer and bowl, and scurried away to his other duties.

In the pantry Bernard and Dickon were waiting to bear in the meats. Nicholas picked up a dish of capons with which he was to lead the procession. It was so heavy that he was only just able to carry it with dignity, and he was thankful to set it on the chest and take up his knife. He had been trained by his mother to hold the joint with his left hand and wield the knife with the right; to touch the meat with the right hand was the worst of bad manners. Thanks to his preparation the ducks and capons were no trouble, but the boar's head, the pasties and legs of Cotswold mutton all had to be sliced and smothered with rich spiced sauces till the trenchers could hold no more, and Bernard and Dickon carried them away to the table.

When everyone had been served and he was free to take his own platter to his appointed place he was worn out and his appetite had forsaken him. He had paid a short visit to the kitchen too, where the heat from the open fire had made him gasp and beat a hasty retreat. He wondered how Peter the cook, the two cook maids, and the scullion boy endured it. The opening in the kitchen roof, which carried away some of the steam and smell and smoke, did not admit any air. However, during the brief moment when he had put his head round the door they all seemed very lively, bustling about and basting the birds on the spits, with hot fat from long-handled spoons held at arm's length. The scullion really had the best of it, for whenever he could be spared from turning the spits, he at least got a breath of fresh air as he carried dirty pots and pans to the back door for the dogs to lick clean, ready to be scoured later with sand and dried bracken.

Nicholas sat on his stool with his supper, and poked at the leg of a capon with his knife. He felt disinclined to touch the greasy meat with his fingers. Dickon filled his goblet with French wine – a treat, for he was allowed only ale as a rule. He drank down the sharp clean liquor with a gulp that brought tears to his eyes. But he felt better for it.

At the centre of the table his father, between the two Lombards, leaned a little wearily against the high back of his chair and listened to Messer Antonio, who, with much elegant play of hands decked with rings, was lecturing Mistress Fetterlock on the wonders of Italian painters. Toad-face, on the contrary, sat in silence, his flabby lips compressed, gazing round the room with an appraising eye – like a dealer at a fair setting his price on everything, thought Nicholas suddenly. All that Giles had said about Lombards came rushing back to his mind, and with it an uneasy fear that something was wrong. The feeling passed, however, when Bernard set a platter of custard and pink jelly before him, and a silver spoon to eat it with. He tasted it. Um! it was good. He settled down again happily.

The jelly was barely finished when the sound of a horse's hooves on the cobbles outside caught his ear. His mother heard it too. He saw her peering through the uneven panes of the window to discover who it could be riding up to the front of the house. Her colour changed. She half rose from her chair, sat down again, then whispered to Bernard, and sent him hurrying towards the door.

But before he could reach it, it was flung open, and a man strode ceremoniously into the hall.

*

He was a tall man with a ruddy face. He halted for an instant as he saw the party at the table, pulled off his hat, flung back his riding cloak, and, smiling cheerfully, swept a deep bow.

'On my soul,' he exclaimed, 'I seem to have burst in upon a feast. Madam, my sister, a thousand pardons. Most worshipful sir, I am your mastership's most humble servant.'

Nicholas jumped to his feet. This was his mother's brother, John Stern, his favourite uncle, a Bristol sea-captain, full of rich salty fun, and thrilling stories. Some of his tales were certainly true, and others, so wild that they were probably just sailor's yarns, nevertheless held the exciting possibility that they might prove to be true after all.

Mistress Fetterlock greeted her brother with as much enthusiasm as a gentlewoman should bestow upon a kinsman, but with very little more. Nicholas realized at once that she was displeased and wished that Master Stern had come at any other time. His father, on the other hand, was genuinely glad. Another place was laid, Bernard carried away the cloak and the cap, and Nicholas, prompted by his mother, waited upon his uncle with the silver ewer and bowl.

John Stern looked at him quizzically, one busy eye-brow shot up at an angle.

'What is this?' he demanded. 'Am I to lap like a puppy? To *wash*? By cock and pie, boy, that's no use to me. If I'm to wash show me the water-trough.'

Gladly Nicholas led the way, stood by to catch the doublet his uncle tossed to him, and watched while he sluiced head and hands, splashing the water over his mop of wiry grizzled hair.

Uncle John at the water-trough

He explained, as he rubbed himself on a coarse kitchen towel, that he was riding from Bristol to London. He had a matter of importance to put before the King's officers. He grinned as he caught his nephew's questioning eye. No! It was not  piracy again. This time he was running after the King's officers, not the King's officers after him. But, he added warningly, not a word to the worshipful company in the hall. If Nicholas was a good lad and kept his tongue quiet for the present, he should hear all about it later on. And now for some food. He was as hungry as a hunter.

The first course was finished when they got back to the table, and the meal was about to begin all over again with the second course. Nicholas's task of handing the washing bowl between the two courses had been performed in his absence by Dickon. Nicholas had never been able to understand why rich people had two or even three courses, since each course was a complete meal in itself, meat, poultry, fish, pastry, and sweetmeats. Going back to the beginning was like starting another dinner. It seemed silly. Why did not people eat as much as they wanted in the first place? Poor people, like Giles and Meg, had only one course, often only one dish.

However on this occasion it worked out very well. John Stern took the seat placed for him next to his sister and made up for missing the first course by devouring double portions of the second. He ate greedily, cramming the food into his mouth and sucking the gravy noisily from his fingers, greatly to the discomfiture of Mistress Fetterlock, who chattered brightly and nervously to distract the attention of the company. Nicholas felt sorry for his mother. She set so much store by table manners, and had always insisted that he cut his meat instead of tearing it with his fingers, and did not pick his teeth at table, or throw the bones on the floor.

John Stern was looked upon as the black sheep of the family, though nowadays he had become part owner of a fleet of respectable merchant ships based on the port of Bristol and trading with Dublin and France and Spain. In days gone by, however, he had sailed a small privateer, the *Katharine* of Dartmouth, in which he plied up and down the Channel carrying wool and leather and cloth to the foreign ports and bringing back salt and wines and silks. The *Katharine* had been armed. In those troublous days all shipmasters were permitted to carry arms, and he and his crew, like other privateers, were always eager to strike a blow at any vessel belonging to a hostile country. If the enemy ship had a cargo which could be seized as a prize of war, so much the better. The prospect of pickings was enough to goad on the crew, and if the spoils were not strictly legal what matter? If they stole a Frenchman's goods, his countrymen would return the compliment as soon as they got the chance.

As tempers grew hotter, the rulers of all the countries concerned tried to stop this piracy. King's ships patrolled the seas. But the pirates were too many for them, and the temptation of rich prizes made the raiders both cunning and bold. The best of them preyed only upon enemies, but others plundered friend and foe alike with such cruelty and ferocity that honest men scorned the name of 'privateer'. It was a great relief to Mistress Fetterlock when her brother sold the *Katharine* and settled down in the rich and respectable trading port of Bristol.

Nicholas could see that she was not pleased when Uncle John, warmed by food and wine, launched upon the sort of stories that he himself loved best. Some of them were new and thrilling, but others were just old favourites often told, such as the story of the pirate Harry Pay of Poole, who, with his one little ship, had actually raided the coast of Spain and carried off the great crucifix on Cape Finisterre as a trophy.

The Lombards listened in silence, and their host, noticing the expression on their faces, tried to head the conversation into safer channels. It was common knowledge that the Italian galleys which sailed from Genoa and Venice to English and Flemish ports, laden with silks and jewels and precious spices, were specially marked down for attention by roving pirates. Messer Antonio remained suave and unruffled, but the secretary's face grew red and angry.

He leaned forward to speak from the length of the table to John Stern.

'Is your mastership familiar with the Isle of Wight?' he asked, speaking with a clear deliberation which made the casual question sound very important.

John Stern seemed taken aback.

'I have been there,' he said non-committally. 'But it was many years since. There is good shelter, and the drinking water of the island keeps fresh on a voyage longer than any I have met.'

Toad-face persisted.

'I have no doubt that a gentleman of your calling must know the harbour of Newport?' Even to Nicholas it was clear that these questions meant something more than appeared on the surface.

John Stern squared his shoulders. 'Good sir,' he returned, somewhat sharply. 'Hap be I do know the harbour of Newport. It is my business to know every harbour of this land, much as it seems yours to infest the mart of every town.'

It was rude; worse than rude, it was an insult, and Nicholas wondered why his uncle should answer so churlishly. He saw Messer Antonio's gown part as his hand slipped inside to the jewelled handle of a dagger in his girdle. Toad-face sprang to his feet, his fingers closing on a table knife. But Master Fetterlock interrupted, pouring wine into the Lombards' cups and changing the subject. The adventurers who interested him the most, he declared, were those gallant captains who explored unknown seas; such men as the Portuguese, Bartolomeo Diaz, who had recently sailed south along the coast of Africa and actually round the Cape of Storms till he faced to the north again. It was said that the King of Portugal had renamed the Cape of Storms and called it the Cape of Good Hope. Did Messer Antonio know if that was true?

Recovering himself the Lombard withdrew his hand from his girdle and lifted his goblet instead. Evidently he too wished to avoid a quarrel, for he took the hint and passed from stories of the Portuguese Diaz to the feats of the great Venetian Messer Marco Polo who nearly two centries ago had reached Cathay, the land of the famous Kublai Khan, with the wonderful cities of Suchow and Peking, and had opened up trade routes which merchants from his own beloved Florence had followed ever since.

The crisis was past, and Mistress Fetterlock, who had

been looking more and more anxious, beckoned to Nicholas and told him in a whisper to fetch her lute. He obeyed reluctantly, for he knew what was going to happen. His mother was going to require him to sing to her accompaniment. He hated singing in public. However there was no help for it, so he did his best and sang '*Ave Maris Stella*', pronouncing his Latin neatly and carefully, as Master Richard, the priest, had taught him. Messer Antonio watched him, with the old genial half smile, and praised him at the end. Then both the Italians pleaded for a song from his mother. Mistress Fetterlock yielded coyly, and sang 'The Nut-Brown Maid', a very long English ballad, with which Messer Antonio described himself as enchanted. The awkward corner had been turned, and everyone was friendly again. The feast came to an end. Nicholas took round his ewer and bowl yet once more – this time a very necessary business, since all fingers were sticky with food. Then with full ceremony Mistress Fetterlock withdrew to her bower, attended by Nicholas carrying her lute, her cushion, and her napkin.

Once out of earshot this elaborate parade came to an abrupt end. She folded back her skirt and headed for the kitchen to see what the servants were doing with the remains of the food.

Nicholas she dispatched to bed.

Chapter 5

SAILS TO THE WEST

It was a hot night for so early in the year. Nicholas lay
on his back, and through the window glass watched the
moon rise. He did not want to go to sleep before his
uncle came up, for he hoped to hear some more stories.
His uncle would be certain to share his bed because the
great chamber, reserved for guests, would be occupied
by the Lombards, and, in any case, it was more usual for
John Stern to be bidden to sleep with his nephew than
for the ceremonial bed to be opened for him.

It was not hard to keep awake. Nicholas was restless.
The straw of his mattress pricked him all over and
made him itch; at least he presumed that it was the
straw. It might be fleas, but his mother was very particular about fleas. Every spring she declared a regular
war against them, setting traps with slices of bread
smeared with bird lime and turpentine, on which the
fleas stuck fast. Indeed all through the year she stood
over the maidservants while they shook the bedding on
to rough white blankets where the fleas were easy to see
and almost as easy to catch. But for all her care no one

could expect to have no fleas at all, and
at this moment Nicholas felt as if armies
of them were hopping all over him. He
punched his straw bolster, vainly hoping
to make it softer. His father and mother
had a feather bed and feather pillows,
but he'd have to be grown up and
married before he could expect to sleep
on feathers. His mother believed that
children should be brought up in a
hard school. When *she* was young, she
informed him, her brothers had been
given a log of wood to rest their heads
upon.

*The little statue
on a carved
wall bracket*

The moonlight crept round the room
till it rested on the little statue of the
Holy Mother and Child which stood on
a carved wall bracket opposite the bed.
Remembering that he'd scrambled over
his night prayers, Nicholas said an *Ave*
to himself, and turned over in bed
so that the air cooled his bare back. He
must have dozed, for by the time that footsteps and
voices outside roused him, the moonlight had reached
the door.

His father was escorting the guests to the great chamber. He could hear the exchange of good nights. A few
minutes later the door of the room opened and his
uncle came in.

He carried a lighted taper, but almost immediately
blew it out, as though he feared that he might wake his
nephew.

'I'm not asleep,' Nicholas announced quickly.

'Small wonder,' said his uncle, adding a salty oath

which Nicholas stored in his memory for future use. 'This room is like an oven. For the love of all the saints, let us have some air.'

He crossed to the window, threw open the casement and stood by it in the moonlight, his burly figure chequered in black and white. Nicholas sat up, enjoying the flood of scented air. His mother hated open windows. Rooms were aired when they were cleaned, she argued, in her practical way; but, having paid for glass windows, through which you could get light without letting in cold air, why open them? Glass was too great a luxury to be treated with such contempt. If you were fortunate enough to live in a house with glass windows, it was stupid to behave as though you lived in a cottage which had none.

John Stern turned back into the room.

'In the name of heaven, boy,' he began, 'whence came those villainous rogues to this house?'

From the darkness of the bed Nicholas stared at him. 'Do you mean the Lombards?' he said. 'I know not whence they came. My father met them in Oxford, so they told me. He bade them come here to sup.'

'He might as well bid the devil as he is about it,' growled Master Stern. He sat down on the coffer at the end of the bed, and, dragging off a boot, kicked it angrily across the room. Obviously he was bursting with pent-up wrath and here was his nephew only too ready to listen. What was Nicholas's father thinking of to entertain these pestilent usurers? he demanded. A boy of Nicholas's age might not know what these Italian robbers were like, but a Merchant of the Staple could not be in ignorance.

'What do they *do*?' asked Nicholas anxiously.

'Do? They ride the country, stealing trade out of

honest men's hands, and then lending again, at huge interest, the
money they have snatched so
villainously. I tell you, nephew,
they are the curse of this modern
world – worse than the black
plague! They taint every business
with their *florins* – yes we are even
adopting the coins that bear the
name of their city, Florence!'

Nicholas sighed. He had suddenly
remembered the kindly humorous
smile of Messer Antonio, and the
friendly way he had held his arm
when they strolled together in the
garden. Surely Messer Antonio
could not be like the black plague
even if Toad-face was.

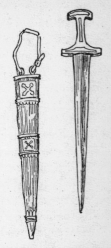

*The Anelace, sharp and
double-edged*

Uncle John almost snorted. 'You are easily beguiled,
boy. I'd rather have a devil clad in fiery scales than a
devil clad in silk. That misshapen little varlet of a
secretary at any rate looks what he is, but your oily
smiling merchant prince is the more dangerous of the
two.' He yawned suddenly. 'Ay de mi, I'm sick of these
Lombard usurers – one can't get away from them anywhere. It's maybe no business of mine, but I mightily
fear it bodes no good to find them here, feasted by your
father.'

He flung his garments in the direction of the clothes
horse. Then, clad only in shirt and hose, he went back
to the window to unbuckle from his belt his *anelace*, the
sharp double-edged knife, like a broad short sword, which
every man wore when he went upon a journey. He
slid the blade from its sheath and tested both its edges

carefully with his thumb, while Nicholas, fascinated, watched the steel glinting in the moonlight.

Satisfied, John Stern slipped it home again, and carrying it round to the far side of the bed, laid it on a stool beside his pillow. Though not a word was said, the action was not lost upon Nicholas. He had not forgotten how, downstairs at the supper table, Messer Antonio's hand had flown to his dagger. Certainly if Uncle John and the Lombards were left together for long, there might be bloodshed.

This reminded him of something else.

'Uncle John,' he inquired suddenly. 'Why were you so angry when the Lombard asked if you were familiar with the harbour of Newport?'

His uncle gave a short laugh. 'I was angry, my boy, because he meant to anger me. Newport is a pirate's bolt-hole, used by the most rascally privateers to victual their ships and land their spoils. There are men in Newport who trade in pirates' booty. Even the Steward of the Island has had a hand in it. To ask a mariner in that tone of voice if he were familiar with Newport is as good as to call him a pirate to his face.' He paused a moment, whistled a little tune under his breath, and then said casually, 'Of course I knew my way up the river to Newport well enough when I was a lad, but that was years ago. I'm a sober ship-master of Bristol now, and a member of the Company of Merchant Adventurers, I'd have them know.'

The coverlet heaved, and the cross ropes on which the mattress was laid creaked as he climbed into bed. Nicholas hitched himself more firmly to his side to avoid slipping down-hill.

'Are you really riding to London to see the King?' he asked eagerly. 'You did promise that you'd tell me.'

Uncle John, free of his clothes, was indulging in a comfortable scratch. 'A plague on you, boy. Must you have all that tonight?' he grumbled. 'Ah well, I suppose a promise is a promise. But, mark you, it is for your ear only. Now that he is hand in glove with these rascally Lombards, I shall not even tell your father. It is perfectly true that I am riding to see the King, though it's more than likely that I'll be fobbed off with the King's officers. I am after money, and I'm told that it is easier to wring water from a stone than money from Henry Tudor. There are four of us in this: John Cabot, his son Sebastian, Richard Ameryk, and myself, all ship-masters of Bristol. We want from the King a commission to sail west into the setting sun until we reach the shores of the Indies.'

*

The moonlight had swept right round the room and streamed across the bed before Nicholas went to sleep.

His brain was seething with the excitement of all that Uncle John had told him. He'd vaguely heard of voyages to find wonderful islands – the Isle of St Brandan, or the island of Brazil, but he'd never paid much attention. It was all so far away from Burford. But here was Uncle John actually planning to sail in his own ship to the Indies and Cathay and all those wonderful lands that they had been talking about at supper. It had all suddenly become real and alive with a vengeance.

There was an idea afoot to reach Asia by sailing to the west. Mariners had been talking about it for quite a long time. After all, the world was said to be round, like an apple, and if a ship were to sail westward, across the unexplored ocean, it must sooner or later reach the East Indies and the eastern shores of Asia.

Out in the ocean lay a number of islands. The Portuguese had discovered and taken possession of some – the Canary Isles, the Azores, Madeira. But, it was said, there were others, and bigger ones too. According to sailors' yarns and old legends, far to the west of Ireland lay the Isle of St Brandan, and the great Island of Brazil, which was reputed to be half-way between Europe and Asia. The strange part was that, though everyone had heard of this Island of Brazil, no one had actually seen it, because no one who had landed there had returned to tell the tale. Year after year sailors from Bristol, and other ports, cruised as far westward as they could, and worked back on a zigzag course, yet none of them had found it.

But now there was a sea captain, called Cristoforo Colombo, who had been in Bristol some years back – *he* had a plan for sailing directly to the west, not bothering about islands but going on and on until he came to the East Indies themselves, those wonderful lands of Asia, about which Marco Polo, the Venetian, had written.

This Cristoforo Colombo was a fine seaman. Uncle John knew him well, and his brother Bartolomeo too. He'd once been on a voyage to Iceland with them. Since those days Colombo had been moving about Europe trying to get someone to pay for an expedition; three ships fitted out for a year was what he wanted. He'd even sent his brother to England to ask King Henry. It was a fine chance. But the King was so slow. By the time that he had made up his mind Colombo had got his ships from Spain. It was nearly a year since he had set sail. Perhaps he'd reached the Indies by now, but more likely he was at the bottom of the sea.

Here the really exciting part of the story began. Uncle John told it only after Nicholas had begged and

prayed him to go on.
Before he began he
got out of bed, tip-
toed across to the
closed door and, to
satisfy himself that
there were no eaves-
droppers outside,
flung it suddenly
open.

'Why did you do
that?' Nicholas ask-
ed, as his uncle re-
turned to bed.

'Because your
house is full of
Italians. And this
that I'm telling you
is a secret not to be
whispered within a

He tiptoed across to the door

bowshot of any Italian. Even the seas are alive with
them. Colombo himself is an Italian, and so is Master
Cabot and his sons, though they do now lie at Bristol
and vow themselves good Englishmen. But if yonder
long-nosed moneylender got wind of what I have here
under my pillow, I'd as like as not get a knife in my
back.'

'What is it?' whispered Nicholas, greatly impressed
and straining his eyes to see in the shadows the outline
of the pillow beneath his uncle's head.

But John Stern would not say. He only laughed and
went on with his story.

Some weeks ago an old sailor had come to see him on
board his ship as he lay in harbour at Bristol. The man

was Irish, from Dingle Bay, which was much farther west even than Bristol. He claimed that he had actually seen the Island of Brazil. Sailing from Dingle with a small crew he had landed on the island, which was in truth a land of plenty, with beasts and fruit and water to supply food and drink without limit. On the way back the Irishmen had been attacked by pirates and the old man was the only one to reach home. But he saved the charts of the island. He had brought them to Bristol and John Stern had bought them from him – at a King's ransom, the old rascal. Guided by those charts it should be quite easy to sail to Brazil, refit the ships with fresh food and water there. Starting already half-way across the ocean, they might even now be the first to reach the Indies or the coasts of Asia, and seize for Englishmen some of the fabulous wealth from trade in silks and spices and precious stones which the Italians had claimed for their cities.

Nicholas was so thrilled that he could not think of going to sleep. In vain did his uncle remind him that it must be long after midnight. Even the promise that he should actually see the charts in the morning could not satisfy him. Long after heavy snores announced that John Stern was asleep, Nicholas still sat up, hugging his knees.

The old folk hobbling back to the Almshouses

Chapter 6

IT IS DECREED

HE was sleeping so soundly in the morning, however, that his mother had to shake him before he could wake up. As if in a dream he heard her warn him that the church clock had struck a quarter before seven, and, if he did not hurry, he would be too late to hear Mass. Even then he did not get up at once, but stared at Uncle John who had rolled over and was snoring again. He heard her leave the house before he tumbled out of bed. Of course it was the proper thing for all who could to go to Mass every morning, but he did wish that, just for once, he dared to stay between the sheets.

It was so late he had to run all the way down the hill. Luckily it was not his turn to serve at the altar or he would have had sharp words from Master Richard, the parson. Mass had begun when he arrived at the church; he caught a glimpse of the priest's vestments, red for Whitsuntide, through the carved Rood screen. The congregation were clustered in little groups at the

The Brass commemorating his grandparents

various points from which they could best see the altar, with a larger group near the doors, ready to slip out quickly to their daily work.

Nicholas joined his father, who stood against a pillar. His mother occupied one of the few carved benches in the centre of the church, with a cushion for her knees. At the opposite end of the bench kneeled Master Antonio Bari, his fur-lined gown pulled round him against the chill of the English morning. He was staring down, Nicholas noted with satisfaction, at the large brass commemorating another Nicholas Fetterlock and wife, his own grandparents. The two figures, lying full length, beneath a triple canopy, showed his grandfather as a young man, his feet resting on a wool-pack, and his grandmother, wearing an old-fashioned horned head-dress, with a little dog just like Bel lying on her skirts. There was a Latin inscription beginning 'Hic jacet Nicolus Fetterlock', 'Here lies Nicholas Fetterlock', and the canopy was decorated with the Fetterlock merchants' mark. It was the finest brass in the church and Nicholas was proud of it.

The tinkle of a bell at the altar recalled his attention. His father had dropped to his knees, and Nicholas followed suit, wishing heartily, as the stone struck cold through his hose, that he had put on a long cote, as his father had. Then, as another bell announced the solemn moment of the Mass, he bowed his head and prayed.

*

When it was all over he waited outside for his mother, to carry her books and her cushion, as she liked him to do. She was very devout, and while she lingered to light a taper before the altar of St Catherine, her patron saint, he perched on the churchyard wall and watched the old folk from the almshouses, built by the great Earl of Warwick, hobble past him, finish their morning gossip and go in to break their fast. It was a lovely morning, so still that he could hear the bleating of sheep and the jangle of sheep-bells, down by the river where the washing was going on. That meant that Giles and Hal and the others had started work on the ewe flock. He himself had helped to fasten the bells round the necks of the ewes. He wished to goodness that he could go and join them but there was not much time to spare before he must be at the parsonage for his lessons with Master Richard.

There had been a great to-do about Nicholas's education. When he was small he was sent to a chantry school, founded by a wealthy wool-man for ten poor boys who were to be taught by the chantry priest and to pray for the soul of their benefactor. His mother had objected strongly. She did not wish her son to be mistaken for a poor boy; but his father brushed the objections aside. He paid fees for Nicholas, and so provided the means for some more needy scholar. So Nicholas wore the habit of the chantry school, until he outgrew its simple teaching.

Then the same to-do broke out afresh. His mother wished to send him as a page to a noble house or, failing that, to one of the Oxford colleges. He could go when he was fourteen, or perhaps even before. But his father said No very firmly. The boy was neither a gentleman of coat armour nor a learned clerk, but just a simple merchant's son who had his business to learn. If he were sent away it must be to London where he could be apprenticed in the trade like any other lad. The argument ended in compromise. Nicholas could remain at home, apprenticed to his own father, but he should go for lessons to the parson, *Master* Richard Chaunccellor, a learned man who had studied at Oxford University. The title 'Master', when used for a priest, in itself signified that he held the degree of Master of Arts. Otherwise he would be addressed simply as 'Sir', like *Sir* John Tucker at Netherfield or *Sir* Peter Stubb at Wold, both worthy priests, no doubt, but untutored except in their church books. It was fortunate for Nicholas that they had at Burford such a parson as Master Richard, who already taught one or two of the sons of well-to-do burgesses of the town.

*

It seemed to Nicholas as if his mother would never come out of church.

But at last she emerged followed by Master Antonio Bari. Nicholas received from the Lombard her cushion and Prymer, the new copy, printed on paper at the press in Oxford, not hand-scribed as the old one had been.

He then fell into step behind them, avoiding his mother's eye. He knew that she was hiding Bel beneath her clock, carefully concealed from Master Richard who had strong views about fashionable ladies bringing their pet dogs to church. Bel's sharp nose emerged from between the folds and Nicholas quickly looked the other way. He did not want to carry the yapping little beast.

Messer Antonio's beautiful manners were as flowery as ever, despite the chill of the morning. As they strolled up the hill he held forth about the virtue of the English, their piety and their devotion. He had been told of it, he declared, by his old friend Messer Trevisian, a Venetian, who knew the country well. But now he was privileged to see it with his own eyes. Mistress Fetterlock accepted the tribute gracefully, but Nicholas, this time, was not so sure. Uncle John's words echoed in his head: 'Your oily smiling merchant prince –' Was Uncle John right? Was Messer Antonio too good to be true? He was glad, when they reached the house, to leave the grown-ups in the hall, helping themselves to slices from a boar's head well brawned, while he, in the pantry, washed down hunks of bread and cheese with plenty of sweet cider.

He had barely finished this meal when Uncle John crept in, finger to lips. He had slept late, he said, and their masterships the moneylenders were breaking their fast in the hall. He'd like a cup of ale here, if Nicholas could find him one.

Delighted, Nicholas filled a large mug from the cask in the buttery and set it before his uncle, at the same time reminding him about the old sailor's chart of the island of Brazil. John Stern needed little prompting. Willingly enough he produced from inside his doublet a slim roll of parchment, guarded in a sheath of silk. When Nicholas, at his bidding, had made sure that the doors were all shut, he unrolled it tenderly and spread it upon the trencher board, held down by mugs and platters and rolls of bread.

At first Nicholas could make little of it. Only when Uncle John, with a horn spoon as pointer, traced the course of an imaginary ship, did he grasp which was sea and which was land. Thus explained by his uncle, it became very exciting. There was, it seemed, a fine sheltered harbour on this island, where the mermaids and the sea serpents and the other dangers were safely left behind. The map showed also the rivers and lakes of fresh water, the groves of sweet fruits and the haunts of birds and animals which could all be taken to replenish the larder of a ship on its way across the Atlantic ocean to the distant coasts of Asia.

Their heads were close together when Nicholas heard his name called. It was his mother's voice. Reluctantly he slipped from his stool and went into the hall.

The Lombards were just going, his mother told him. He must fetch a stirrup cup of wine quickly, and then come and hold their cloaks while they mounted.

Everyone gathered at the front door to see the visitors start: Thomas Fetterlock and his lady, Nicholas, Dickon and Bernard, and all the servants, gaping or peeping from behind window-panes. A little way down the road waited the rest of the cavalcade of yesterday, the baggage horse, the men at arms, the gazehound. Messer Antonio swept a bow nearly to the ground. He protested that he was full of grief at leaving so hospitable a house, but they must hasten to Southampton with all speed for the loading of their galleys. Even the surly Toad-face was fulsome in his thanks. They all drank a toast to their next meeting from the cup that Nicholas carried, and with clatter and cries and jangling harness, they rode away.

Immediately Nicholas attempted to slip back to Uncle John in the pantry. But to his astonishment his father gripped him by the shoulder. He wanted to speak to him, he declared. He had something important to say, and there was no time like the present. If Nicholas were late for his lessons with Master Richard, he would put it right.

Nicholas followed him to the room called the counting-house, where, when he was at home, his father conducted his business. It was a small panelled room, containing a counter-board covered by a carpet, two stools, some shelves holding thick leather-bound ledgers, a small locked coffer, an inkwell, a canister of sand, quills, scissors, a ball of twine, and all the litter of business.

Thomas Fetterlock sat down at the counter-board, resting his elbows upon it, and began absent-mindedly to sweep into little piles, the scattered sand. Nicholas, suddenly frightened, hastily searched his memory for any crime that he might have committed.

Suddenly his father raised his eyes and looked at him.

'You are getting a big boy, my son,' he said. 'Methinks that it is time that you were wed.'

Nicholas gasped. 'Wed?' The single word conveyed all his astonishment and dismay. Marriage was one of those things, like death, that happened to other people, but not to oneself.

'Well, betrothed, then – if you like the word better. It comes to the same thing, since a betrothal, properly contracted, is almost as binding as a marriage. I had been betrothed to your mother for a year when I was your age. You cannot be actually married yet. The bride is too young.'

Nicholas gasped. 'Wed?'

'The bride.' This was worse and worse. Evidently it was already arranged. And who was the bride to be? His mind ran over all the maidens that he knew. Each one seemed worse than the last.

His father, glancing at the boy's white face, patted the stool beside him.

'Her name is Cecily Bradshaw. She lives at Newbury. She is eleven years old, and such a good lively maid that you will not find a better anywhere. Mark you, my son, there shall be no enforcement. If it should hap that, when you know her, you cannot abide her, nor she you, then I will not continue with it, though it cost me all I have. Come and sit beside me, and I will tell you everything.'

Still dazed, Nicholas sat down.

Thomas Fetterlock spoke simply, as though he were explaining to a small child. He began about the Staple. Nicholas knew, he said, that as Thomas Fetterlock, wool trader, he was a member of the Staple, as his father had been before him, and as, he hoped, his son would be after him. The Honourable Fellowship of the Wool Staple was the most powerful of all the trade guilds. It had its headquarters at Calais, the last city of France to remain English. The Staple was responsible for the town. They paid for its garrison and its defence, and kept it in law and order. People said that if the Staple failed, England would lose Calais too.

From Calais the Staple controlled almost all the wool that left England. Not a fleece, not a sarpler of English wool could be sold in France or Flanders – the richest markets in the world – unless it had passed through Calais, and been listed, checked, and priced by the officers of the Staple. True, a small quantity of wool was bought by foreigners, under special licence from the King, but even that wool, though it was already sold, must not go to Flanders without permission of the Staple. All these rules had been excellent when the Staple was governed for the benefit of its three hundred members, but of late years the power had got into the hands of twenty or thirty of the biggest merchants who made laws to suit their own interests.

They fixed the prices, received all the money, and held it for so long that it might be three or four years before the smaller merchants were paid. The result of all this was that the trade was crippled. Now no firm could export more than 300 sarplers of wool a year, whereas in his grandfather's time it had been five times that quantity. Everyone was in difficulties. Even his own business would have been ruined by now if he had not borrowed money from the Lombards.

Nicholas who, since all this seemed to have nothing to do with his betrothal, had been only half-listening, woke up when his father mentioned Lombards.

'The Lombards,' he repeated. 'Oh, sir, do you mean *these* Lombards, Messer Bari and the other one? My uncle said that they were moneylenders.'

'Your uncle talks too much,' his father replied sharply. 'Messer Antonio Bari is the agent of the Medici, who are the most honourable bankers in the world. I am fortunate to deal with him. I'll trouble you to repeat no mischief to me about the Lombards.'

Nicholas, reproved, sat silent, wishing that they could come back to the subject of his marriage. As though reading his thoughts his father suddenly smiled at him.

'Be patient, my son,' he said. 'You may think that this has no bearing upon your betrothal, but I am coming to that now. Have you ever watched weavers making cloth on their looms?'

Surprised, Nicholas said Yes. Many people in Burford had looms set in sheds at the back of their dwelling-houses. One heard the thump and rattle of them as one went down the street.

Master Fetterlock nodded. 'Does that convey anything to your mind? I have told you that, in my view, the outlook for the wool trade is dark. There is one alternative – cloth.'

He paused, and glanced at Nicholas to see if this had sunk in. Then he continued.

Flanders was the home of the great 'clothiers' – the cloth merchants. Flemish weavers bought the best English wool – after it had been through the Staple of course – and made it into cloth which sold all over Europe. They used to have the market to themselves, but nowadays they had the English cloth makers to compete with. That wise old King Edward III had seen, more than a hundred years ago, which way the wind was blowing and had encouraged Flemish weavers and dyers and fullers to settle in England so that Englishmen could learn the secrets of the craft. Gradually the English cloth trade had grown until now it was as big and important as the wool trade – and a great deal more profitable. Raw wool paid a huge export tax. If it was made into cloth it could be exported with hardly any tax at all. Cloth was not controlled by the Staple. The cloth merchants had joined another Guild, the Company of Merchant Adventurers, who carried the cloth all over the world in their own ships.

Nicholas pricked up his ears again. Uncle John had mentioned the Merchant Adventurers.

'So, my son,' his father was saying, 'I am going to form an alliance with a firm of clothiers. I have found a fine and powerful house – the house of Bradshaw of Newbury. Already I am selling wool to them, without tax, mark you, and without having to wait on the whims of their worships of the Staple. With my son wedded to the daughter of Master Edward Bradshaw, we shall have both doors open to us, the cloth trade as well as the wool trade, and the future for you and your children should indeed be bright.'

*

Nicholas left his father half an hour later not sure whether he was on his head or his heels. It had all come upon him so suddenly, like one of those summer storms that broke over the wolds. It did not occur to him to expect any choice in the matter, or even that he had the right to protest. He, and every other boy or girl, so far as he knew, was trained to complete and unquestioning obedience. Any trace of rebellion had been beaten out of him so early that he did not even remember it. Besides parents always arranged their children's marriages, and he was bound to marry some day. The trouble was that it had come upon him so completely without warning.

The betrothal would take place soon. In a few days' time he was to ride to Newbury with his father to meet his future wife. He had never known any girls as he had no sister and all his life he had played with boys. He hated the thought of being tied for good to some prim mincing little milk-sop of a girl.

The one bright spot for him in the whole wretched business was the great Fair held at Newbury on the eve of the feast of Corpus Christi, which would take place during their visit. Newbury Cloth Fair was known throughout the Cotswolds, where all the wool-men loaded their packhorses and headed south, hoping to get orders from the clothiers, who made and sold the cloth. Nicholas loved a fair, though so far he had only been to the small local ones. When his father, to cheer him up, mentioned the Corpus Fair at Newbury, he had at once begged that they might take Hal with them. At that moment his father would have granted him any favour, so he agreed readily enough that Hal should go as Nicholas's personal servant. He would be a rough and ready one, but he could learn from Dickon.

Half in a dream Nicholas climbed the stairs to his bed-chamber to fetch his satchel. He ought, of course, to have been at the parsonage hours ago. On the way up he heard his mother call him from her bower, a large room on the first floor, with a window that looked across the valley. It was cheerful and smelled nice because of the sweet sedge which she always mixed with the floor rushes. The walls had bright hangings and so had the big bed, which during the day was disguised with cushions and became the most comfortable seat in the house. There were also two coffers, both gaily painted, and a prie-dieu, where his mother said her prayers before a lovely little picture of the Nativity which his father had bought in Bruges.

Mistress Fetterlock was busy at her new spinning-wheel when he went in, but she stopped and held out her hand to him. Before he could drop on one knee he drew him towards her, put an arm round him, and kissed him on the cheek. Such tenderness was rare from his mother, and Nicholas, feeling a lump in his throat, hoped desperately that she was not going to say anything to make him cry. But Mistress Fetterlock was always practical. She remarked that his new doublet and gown should arrive from Oxford soon and Nicholas realized suddenly that all these new clothes must have been ordered because of the bethrothal.

Next she produced a beautiful new comfit jar which Messer Antonio had brought her. It was of glazed pottery decorated with scrolls of blue and brown, and a

A new comfit jar

large blue fleur-de-lis which, she said, was the emblem of Florence. It contained candied fruits. She told him to hold out his hand for a sugar plum, and for pity's sake, not to wipe his sticky fingers on his hose.

The sweetmeat was comforting. He slung his satchel over his shoulder and was just leaving the house when he remembered Uncle John. He had left him in the pantry, but he could not still be there. Nicholas hoped he had not gone already, and as a few more minutes could not matter when he was already so late, he went to look for his uncle and found him in the stable-yard, supervising the saddling of his horse.

John Stern grinned at him, clapped him across the shoulders and heartily wished him luck. Obviously he, too, had heard the news. Suddenly Nicholas gripped his uncle's arm.

'Take me with you,' he begged in a hoarse whisper. 'Oh Uncle John, let me come with you.'

'Take you? Where? To London?'

'Ay – to London – anywhere – on the voyage to the Islands or to Asia; I don't care where.'

John Stern burst out laughing. 'Bless the boy, he's running away from his bride. That'll never do. Count yourself lucky, young man. I wish I were your age.'

So there was no help for it, even from Uncle John. Nicholas pulled himself together and set off again for the parsonage, Uncle John's fruity jests ringing in his ears. He had to be content with the promise that Uncle

John would come again on his way back from London, would finish showing him the charts and tell him if he had seen King Henry.

Even now he was not to go straight to his lessons. Half-way down the hill he met Hal, who was on his way to Nash the barber, where he often lent a hand by holding down a patient while a tooth was pulled out or a boil lanced. He could not resist telling Hal the news, and did so with a dash of bravado.

Hal was dumbfounded. 'Wed?' he exclaimed blankly, just as Nicholas had done. 'You?'

As Hal stared at him, his eyes round with astonishment, Nicholas realized suddenly that a barrier would come between the two of them. The old bonds would loosen. There would be fewer and fewer of those long days on the hills with the sheep. Things might never be the same again. Hal – he thought with envy – could at least choose his own wife. He need not marry for years. He need not marry at all if he did not want to. And if he did marry, he would go courting first, as other lads went courting. They had often met courting couples down by the river or through the woods and had treated them to jokes and catcalls, and enjoyed it. Now it dawned on Nicholas that boys of his class did not go courting like that. Their marriages were arranged for them. They had no choice, but were tied up for good and all at their parents' orders and to suit their parents' convenience.

Nicholas struggled to put these ideas away, feeling that he was disloyal. Master Richard would tell him that he was also sinful, since, after his duty to God, his next duty was to honour his father. and mother, and obey them. He knew that well enough, but, as Hal stood silently looking at him, his heart was full of revolt. Once more he was terribly afraid that he might cry, so he said gruffly that he must go.

Only when he had reached the bottom of the hill did he remember that he had not even mentioned Newbury Fair, nor told Hal that he was to come too.

A large stone barn standing by itself

Chapter 7

THE BARN

THE parsonage lay close to the river, where there were plenty of fish. Master Richard enjoyed the fishing, and stored his catch alive in the pond in his garden. It was never empty, and his parishioners always knew where to beg for a fresh trout or a perch or two.

The house was built of stone below and of timber beams above, with a roof of oak shingles from the near-by forest of Wychwood. It had a hall, a little parlour, a sleeping room above and the usual kitchen and buttery, dovecot and barn. It stood in a well-stocked garden, and Master Richard was as generous with his fruit as with his fish. His people loved him for he was their servant from the cradle to the grave. Other parsons might be grudged their tithes, but not Master Richard. The tenth share of his people's harvest was brought to his barn without reminder. The tenth honeycomb and the tenth egg appeared in plenty and more work was put into his glebe fields than the tenth share of what each labourer earned, which was lawfully his due.

Nicholas paused when he reached the hall door and listened. Master Richard was strict with his scholars, and though Master Fetterlock had promised to give his son a written excuse, he had not done so. However the sounds inside the parsonage told him quite certainly that Master Richard was not there – so he lifted the latch and went in.

Two boys were in the hall. One, a big burly youth, Fulk Rollinson, son of the most unpopular man in Burford, the reeve, who collected the King's taxes, was casting dice on the floor, and singing cheerfully a popular song, 'Sweetheart, Have Pity', which would certainly not have met with the approval of Master Richard. The other, a thin white-faced lad, bent over a parchment on which he was illuminating a capital letter with infinite care.

'Where's the Master?' inquired Nicholas, noting the open books upon the lectern.

'Where are your wits?' retorted the big boy. 'Did you not know that there was a wedding at the church door this forenoon? It was your turn to carry the Holy Water too. Master Richard had to take Stephen instead, but they won't be long. It was just in the porch, with no Nuptial Mass afterwards so they'll only go into the church for a blessing from the altar. What happened to you?'

'I forgot,' said Nicholas briefly. In spite of a possible birching from the Master, he was not sorry that he had missed this particular turn. A marriage, with or without ceremony, was the last thing he fancied at the moment. 'What's the task this morning?' he asked.

'Donat, of course,' grumbled Fulk, referring to every schoolboy's bugbear, the Latin Grammar according to Donatus on which so many generations had been reared. 'But I've been learning my "Halter Verses" again. You might hear me say them.'

Nicholas stepped up to the lectern and turned the pages of Master Richard's big Psalter until he reached the 50th Psalm. To be able to read or recite Psalm 50, the 'Miserere', was of great benefit if a man should be charged with any crime, for it was one of the tests by which he could claim to be a 'clerk' – a *cleric* of Holy Church – and therefore entitled to be tried by Church courts instead of by the King's court. As the Church did not condemn anyone to death, the offender might quite literally save his neck from the halter by knowing the verses.

Nicholas nodded as he found the place. 'Say away,' he invited.

Fulk started full tilt at the Latin: 'Miserere mei, Deus –' but after a few verses he came to an abrupt stop.

Nicholas laughed shortly. 'Same old place. You never get past that fourth verse. If your neck depended on your saying the Miserere you'd certainly be hanged.'

Fulk shrugged his shoulders. 'Oh well, I know the first verse, and really it's only the first verse that counts. You can claim Benefit of Clergy if you can repeat that.'

'You'd better not say that to Master Richard,' Nicholas retorted scornfully. 'He'd be pretty angry at the thought of a scholar of his gabbling the first verse to save his neck like any common knave. And anyhow you have to be tonsured before you can claim to be a clerk, you know.' He laughed to himself as he eyed Fulk's unruly crop of tousled hair. Really, it was difficult to imagine Fulk with a neatly shaven crown. 'I doubt whether Master Richard would recommend you for the tonsure. He's strict you know.'

'Oh the tonsure's nothing,' said Fulk loftily. 'They

clip the hair on the top of the head, but it would soon grow again if one wanted it to. Anyhow, a plague on Psalms. Let's throw the dice.'

The invitation passed unheeded. There was something disgusting about the light-hearted way that Fulk was preparing to avoid punishment for crimes which he might commit in the future. Nicholas turned away, and went to look at the work of the other boy, who was poring over his parchment.

'That is wonderful,' he said, gazing at the beautiful even lettering of the page of Scripture that he was copying. '*You* ought to be a clerk, you know.'

The thin boy looked up at him eagerly. 'I want to be a scribe,' he said. 'Master Richard promised to try and get me work at Oxford. It's difficult now, because people are having books printed instead of copied, but there'll always be books for the Church – Missals and Psalters and Gospels. I shouldn't think those would ever be printed, would you?'

Before Nicholas could reply he heard a step on the garden path. Fulk heard it too. The dice went quickly into his pouch and when the priest opened the door he was buried in his Latin Grammar.

Master Richard was a tall spare man, with shoulders that stooped from long hours peering into manuscripts by winter candle-light. His blue eyes were shrewd and his expression stern, until a smile softened his face and bathed it in kindliness. Nicholas stood up, expecting a rebuke, but instead the Master nodded to him genially. Instantly Nicholas realized that Master Richard knew his secret already. In the lesson that followed the priest was lenient with him, asking him easy questions. When it was over and the other boys went home, he signed to Nicholas to remain behind.

Nicholas's heart sank. Was it to be a lecture on the duties of marriage? But if Master Richard knew of the betrothal, he did not refer to it. He had kept Nicholas, he explained, because he had set some eel traps in the river, and wanted to see if they had caught anything. They went out together and Nicholas's spirits rose as if by magic. He loosened his points on the river bank and slipped out of his hose in a trice. The water was cold and he turned up his toes with a shiver as he waded in.

Lessons at the parsonage

By the time the traps were cleared of weed and the eels tipped into the parson's fish pond, he had forgotten all about his worries. He went home with a calm mind and a fine appetite for dinner.

After the formality of last night's feast, the dinner to-day was a simple affair, served for his parents and himself in the dining parlour. There was only one dish – a delicious Hotch Potch, made from all the meats of the night before cooked together in the cauldron. In the presence of his parents no boy was expected to speak unless spoken to, so he addressed himself heartily to his food.

On this occasion, however, the conversation concerned him closely. After dinner he was to ride over to Northleach with Dickon, his father told him.

'To ride?' Nicholas repeated, wondering what he was to ride upon. He had so much outgrown his pony that he felt a figure of fun with his feet stuck out in front to avoid touching the ground. Sometimes he rode his mother's palfrey, but he hated its lady-like amble which swayed gently from side to side. Only as a great treat was he ever permitted to mount his father's Bayard, a powerful bay which carried him on the long journeys to London and Dover.

'Dickon will ride Bayard,' his father replied with deliberation. 'You can ride with him, either in front or on pillion, as you please.' Then, as Nicholas's face fell, a twinkle showed in his father's eye. 'On the way back you will ride your own horse.'

Nicholas dropped his spoon into the stew with a splash that set his mother tut-tutting. His own horse! This was the second shock of the day, and how different from the first!

'You'll need a horse to ride to Newbury,' Master Fetterlock continued, wiping his fingers on his napkin, after picking a bone. 'Anyway it is time you had a mount of your own. Master Midwinter is selling his grey mare, Petronel. He's asking five pounds for her, but she is cheap at the price. She's steady and strong, and about the right size. So I've bought her for you, and you are to fetch her this afternoon.'

*

In an ordinary way he would have hated the ride to Northleach, perched woman-wise upon a pillion behind Dickon. Today it was worth his while to put up with it; but he was quite glad that they met no one on the five-mile stretch except a party of Benedictine monks making their way from Gloucester with their black cowls pulled over their heads as protection from the sun, and a couple of pedlars trudging with their wares who were too hot and weary to raise their eyes.

Pedlars trudging with their wares

Nicholas knew the Midwinter house very well. It stood in the centre of the little town of Northleach, since Master Midwinter was a wool-dealer, not a wool-grower, and he chose a position convenient for his business with the merchants of the Staple and their agents who came from London to buy Cotswold wool. His usual way was to accept their orders for so many sarplers of clipped wool, and so many wool fells, to be delivered to them at the King's beam weigh-house at the Leadenhall in London. After a price had been agreed and a third of it paid to Master Midwinter in cash, he would ride round the wolds, buy the wool from the farmers, have it packed in stout Arras canvas and arrange for drovers and packhorses to carry it to London. Once handed over at the Leadenhall it became the business of the Staple merchants, who had it weighed, paid the taxes, and saw it loaded on to ships to go to Calais. Master Midwinter was always grumbling that it was the big merchants who made the profits, and that he had to wait for the remaining two-thirds of his money until the wool found purchasers abroad, but he seemed to earn a comfortable living for all that. The fine church at Northleach, which was continually being beautified by one or another of its richer parishioners, bore witness to the prosperity of the middlemen in the wool trade.

Bayard, with his double load, came to a standstill outside the house, just as Master Midwinter was waving farewell to a departing guest, a square-set well-dressed man, mounted on a fine chestnut horse, and bearing on his gloved left hand a hooded hawk. It was Master Cely from London, Master Midwinter informed Nicholas as the boy jumped to the ground; a Staple merchant; Nicholas's father must know him. He always took his hawk on his long rides buying wool. It beguiled the dull hours, and if he could offer a bag of game to his inn-keeper of a night, so much the better for his reckoning. He was a shrewd fellow, Cely!

Chattering cheerfully, he led Nicholas within doors. Of course, he said, he knew that he had come to fetch the mare, but there were cakes and ale all ready for him, and Mistress Midwinter would never forgive him if he went away without seeing the children.

In a large nursery they found Mistress Midwinter and her family. There were four children, all young and all noisy. As soon as they saw their father they clamoured for a game, and Nicholas soon found himself on all fours as one of the horses in a tourney, bearing through the lists Ralph Midwinter, aged five, armed with a lance of rolled parchment.

It did not last long, for Master Midwinter, a fat jolly man, soon had to cry for mercy. It was thirsty work too, and the cakes and ale were excellent.

On the way to the stable, Master Midwinter asked

Nicholas found himself on all fours

Nicholas how fared his father? Did his troubles seem less black? 'Tell him not to fret himself over the threats of the Staple,' he said cheerfully. 'Their worshipful masters, the Mayor and Council are a queasy lot, full of hums and haws. They threaten much, but I've seen men in worse pass than your father survive it. And if the Staple *should* expel him, what then? Not the end of the world anyway! Tell him to come to me, and I will sell his wool for him. I'm only a plain wool-man, and not a high and mighty Stapler, but I will see him through. Tell him that from me, boy.'

Nicholas promised to bear the message. He did not

know what it was all about, but it sounded ominous with its talk of threats and expulsion. At another time he would have been alarmed and worried. But the whole matter vanished from his mind when he was brought face to face with Petronel, his very own horse. She was a sturdy little grey mare, with an arched neck and kindly eye. Mistress Midwinter had given him a chip from a sugar loaf for her, and she accepted his attentions graciously, allowing him to mount. Once he was up she indulged in a little harmless dance, but, instructed by Master Midwinter, he talked to her and petted her until she was quiet again. Dickon held a leading rein; not, of course, that he required one, laughed Master Midwinter. Anyone could see that he was a good horseman. It was only a precaution, in case she should realize that she was leaving her old home.

But Petronel behaved beautifully. She responded to Nicholas's touch as if she had carried him all her life, and after a mile or two Dickon agreed to dispense with the leading rein. If she pranced a little at first, Nicholas gentled her and she settled down again.

He was thrilled. It was almost worth while being betrothed for this. About half-way along the road from Northleach he remarked that it was a pity to go straight home, and, though Dickon was doubtful, Nicholas turned the mare's head towards the open wolds. Petronel whinnied with pleasure as she felt the crisp upland grass under her feet.

Nicholas knew the country well. He'd roamed this ridge often with Hal, rounding up sheep. A little to his right lay Snowbottom Dean, where two winters ago he had helped Giles to dig a ewe out of a drift.

On the slope of the next down he saw a large barn, standing all by itself, with no other building in sight. It was new, and the idea suddenly came to him that this must be Leach's fine stone barn, about which Giles had so much to say. He might as well go and have a look at it.

Dickon was now far behind. He felt no particular urge to wander about the wolds, so Nicholas patted Petronel and rode on alone.

The barn was certainly in a desolate spot. He followed the line of the hill and approached it from above. While he was still some way off he noticed a couple of horses tethered at the corner of the building. One of them was unmistakable, even at that distance. It was the piebald mare always ridden by Leach himself. Then he saw that the barn doors were open. He backed Petronel into the shadow of a group of thorn trees as two men appeared from inside. The first was Leach: but at the sight of the second, Nicholas drew a sharp breath. He would have recognized those high black shoulders anywhere. It was Toad-face, the Lombard secretary.

The two men stood outside in the sunlight for a couple of minutes examining something which they held in their hands. Then they went back into the barn.

Nicholas seized the opportunity; he turned the mare's head, and went back by the way he had come, keeping the clump of thorn trees between himself and the barn. He did not want to be caught spying upon Leach. But he was troubled. The Lombards had left early in the morning, professing to be in haste to reach Southampton. Yet here, late in the day, was Toad-face, no more than a couple of miles away, and in company with Leach the packer. Remembering Giles's warning, he feared that there was no good in it.

Should he tell his father? He would like to, but his

father thought the world of Leach. He also remembered, a little bitterly, his father's words that morning: 'I'll trouble you to repeat me no mischief against the Lombards.' It was not easy to decide.

That night he attempted to deliver Master Midwinter's message, but he got only as far as the first part: 'Tell him not to fret himself over the threats of the Staple.' At that his father caught him up irritably.

'Threats? What threats? Master Midwinter babbles like a woman. Who said there were threats?'

That question Nicholas was unable to answer. He took refuge in silence. About Leach and the Lombard he said nothing at all.

Coffers ransacked

Chapter 8

THE JOURNEY

Two days later they set out for Newbury.

For Nicholas the days were so busy that they passed in a flash. There was no time to think of Leach, or Lombards, or of anything other than the ceaseless preparations. The only person who really seemed to enjoy the turmoil was his mother. She was in her element, fussing over his new clothes, putting up little wooden bowls of home-made scented soap, filling a leather flask with tooth wash and another with perfumed oil for his hair.

Then Hal must be provided for. As Nicholas's servant he must look respectable. Mistress Fetterlock said this a little sharply. She did not approve of Hal's inclusion in the party. But Meg was summoned, and came, her blue eyes anxious, bearing the few worn and patched garments of rough homespun which comprised Hal's outfit. These were promptly brushed aside by Mistress Fetterlock, and the biggest coffers ransacked to find something that would do – a difficult task since Nicholas's old clothes were too small and his father's too big. In the end a doublet of Master Fetterlock's, with the trimming ripped off it, and a large pair of hose, were thrust into a cauldron of dye and boiled until they were reduced to the right size and to a most suitable dull russet hue. She even found time to embroider on the sleeve in scarlet thread, the Fetterlock merchant's mark. Hal was dispatched to his uncle, the barber, with instructions that his mop of hair should be well plastered down with water and trimmed evenly under a bowl. When in the fresh dawn of a June morning he appeared at the door with Dickon and the horses and the cloaks and the baggage, he looked so neat and subdued and unlike himself, that Nicholas scarcely knew him.

By the time the farewells were finished the sun was well up and throwing long shadows across the dewy grass. As they walked their horses up the hill, and out over the open wolds, Nicholas felt for the first time a little throb of pleasure. If, a week ago, someone had told him that he would soon be riding with his father on his own horse to Newbury Fair, with Hal for company, he would have thrilled with excitement. Yet now he was too full of the sense of change and the dread of an unknown future to be able to enjoy it completely.

All the same it was a perfect morning. To while away the time Master Fetterlock settled down to talk about the Bradshaw family. Mistress Cecily was not, as Nicholas was, an only child. She had several brothers and sisters. One, Walter, about fourteen or fifteen, was a student at Oxford. Cecily was the eldest girl. There was a younger boy and two little sisters. They lived in an old manor house, Beechampton Manor, just outside Newbury Town. It had come to Master Bradshaw through his wife, Cecily's mother, a lady of coat armour. The house was her childhood's home. Master Bradshaw had enclosed a fine park with an oak fence all round it. Though he was a clothier and had made his fortune by his trade, it seemed that he rather enjoyed being Lord of the Manor in his wife's right. Master Fetterlock chuckled gently to himself, as though amused at other men's pleasures. 'Anyway,' he remarked to Nicholas, 'in the future, my boy, you will have no cause to be ashamed of your wife's parentage.'

Nicholas listened intently. This description of the Bradshaw family made everything seem more real. Up to now he had known no more about his bride-to-be than what his father had told him that first day. He supposed that it would all have to be faced at the end of the journey, but in the meanwhile he might as well enjoy the ride.

The road, in places, was scarcely more than a grassy track, with hardened ruts suggesting that in winter it must be deep in mud. It sloped gently downhill as they left the Cotswolds behind them, and descended into the leafy depths of the Thames valley.

Here, through meadows deep in buttercups and ox-eyed daisies, they had to ride single file.

'One would never think,' Thomas Fetterlock remarked over his shoulder, 'that this is quite an important road. It leads to Radcot Bridge, where barges are loaded for Oxford and for London. It's a bad

Radcot Bridge

stretch in the winter – sticky clay, and ample cover for robbers.'

Glancing round him at the tangle of wlilows growing everywhere, Nicholas could well believe it. He wore, for the first time in his life, an anelace slung from his belt, and, even on this sunny morning, he was glad to think of its broad sharp blade.

They plodded on at a walking pace, while the sun rose high in the heavens. Once they turned aside to hear Mass at a tiny village church, whose walls inside were completely covered with paintings, and the roof and arches with silver stars on a blue background, all very bright and gay. There seemed to be only a few cottages in the village, which was no more than a clearing in the wilderness.

A little farther on they came to an alehouse, just a simple thatched cot, with a bush tied to a pole to proclaim its trade. Master Fetterlock ordered a halt. It was three hours since they left home, and it was getting hot. Everyone was glad to rest. They lay about on a shady bank while the good wife brought cool ale in a brown pitcher. She apologized that she had no cakes to offer, but it was baking day, and she had but now lighted the faggots to heat the oven.

It did not matter about the cakes, for Mistress Fetterlock had furnished each of them with a pasty wrapped in a napkin. The woman told them that it was not much more than a bow shot to the river. Once on the other side the road was better and they would get along more quickly.

They crossed the Thames at Radcot by an ancient bridge with three pointed arches, its stones worn by many winter floods.

'A fine bridge, to the honour of our Lady,' observed Master Fetterlock. 'Notice the statue, Nicholas – there, on the side facing downstream. They say this bridge has stood for a couple of hundred years or more, and I should not wonder if it stands another two hundred. A battle was fought here once, when some of the nobles took arms against the Lord King – the second Richard it was, I think. You've been to school since I have, boy.'

But Nicholas could not remember the battle. He did not learn about English battles, only Roman ones, and anyway he was more interested in looking at the river. It hadn't the same sparkle as their own Windrush, he remarked to Hal, as they rode their horses into the shallows to drink. All the same he'd be glad enough to bathe in it, if they had the time.

But, Bayard satisfied, Master Fetterlock had already turned back towards the road, and Nicholas reluctantly followed. To his astonishment he saw a man running along beside his father. Though the sun was in his eyes, he could see the habit of a friar – though where a friar could have come from he did not know. There had been no one in sight when they went down to the river.

'Alms for the bridge, good sir,' the man was shouting. 'Of your charity, alms for the upkeep of the bridge.'

To Nicholas's astonishment, after one glance downwards, his father shook Bayard's rein and rode quickly on. It was strange, because in any pious cause his father was the most generous of men. The friar swung quickly round and almost flung himself in front of Petronel.

'Alms for the bridge,' he cried again. 'Alms for the Holy Hermit. The prayers of the Hermit shall go with you, young master. Day and night shall prayers follow you.'

Uncertain and embarrassed Nicholas looked down at the man's dirty and unshaven face. It did not look very holy, but he spared a hand from Petronel to finger his pouch. There were some farthings in it. He dropped one in the outstretched hand and hurried after his father.

'Did you give him anything?' inquired Master Fetterlock as he caught up. 'A farthing? Well, that won't do any harm. These rogues calling themselves hermits are the plague of the land. I had a mind to bid him show his licence. Every real hermit nowadays has a licence from his bishop. Did you know that, boy? There are plenty of genuine holy men, who give their lives to prayer and fasting, praise be to God. But there are still many impostors who grow fat on the alms they beg.'

'But he was begging for the upkeep of the bridge,' said Nicholas perplexed.

Master Fetterlock laughed. 'A ready plea. Of course most bridges are the business of the Church, and their upkeep is an act of piety. But they are not left to the mercy of chance beggars. Methinks Radcot Bridge is in the Manor of Faringdon, which belongs to the White Monks of Beaulieu, near Southampton.'

'Southampton?' repeated Nicholas. 'Surely that's a long way from Faringdon.'

'A very long way,' said his father. 'The Abbey of Beaulieu is in the New Forest. I have been there often, and you may have heard me speak of it. The white monks are sheep farmers. They have abbeys all over England – Fountains, Furness, Tintern – all sheep districts. Every wool-man knows them. Maybe you'll visit Beaulieu one of these days. Mistress Cecily's grandparents live there, hard by the abbey. They will be your grandparents when you are wed.'

Nicholas turned red. For the moment he had forgotten all about the wedding, and he did not want to be reminded.

'How do the Beaulieu monks come to be in Faringdon?' he asked quickly.

'Somebody bequeathed the Manor to them. They have a house there: my Lord Abbot often visits it. I should venture that they get the corn for the abbey bread from the rich lands round about. They have built at Coxwell near here a barn as big as the abbey church to hold it all. Of course all that does not prove that Radcot Bridge is the monks' care. But I'll wager a silver groat to your farthing that it is not the care of your friend the hermit.'

*

Faringdon was a bustling cheerful little town with two good inns and some stalls in the market-place. Nicholas would have liked to linger and look round, but

Minstrels on their way to the fair

Master Fetterlock said they must press on. They had not yet covered half their journey, and as they neared Newbury the road was likely to be crowded.

Indeed as soon as they left Faringdon they found themselves impeded by other travellers. There were loaded packhorses, rough peasant carts with wattle sides, strong country nags carrying two and sometimes three upon their backs; traders and wool-dealers, well mounted and outstripping the slow traffic; chapmen trudging with packs across their shoulders, all heading south towards Newbury.

Luckily there was a wide stretch of grassland on either side of the road. In these parts, said Master Fetterlock, they abided by the law that undergrowth should be cut back for two hundred feet so as to deny cover to robbers. It was a useful rule because, in addition, it gave fast travellers a chance to pass the slow ones.

By now it was nearly noon, and the sun beat down mercilessly. Nicholas shed first his cloak, then his gown, then his doublet, carrying them flung across his saddle while he rode in shirt, pourpoint and hose. After ten miles of weary jogging they came to Wantage, another market town, and here, Master Fetterlock decreed, they would go to the tavern to dine.

A hot and dejected performing bear

But the tavern was overcrowded and the meat greasy and tough. They remained long enough to rest the horses and thankfully, in spite of the heat, made for the country again. Soon Master Fetterlock left the crowded road and took a bridle path which led to the open downs. Most of the traffic was left behind. Only those who, like themselves, were travelling light could venture up the steep hill-side.

On the top the sun blazed down, but there was a breeze to make the heat bearable. Nicholas looked round him. Though these hills were different from his own wolds, he felt at home on the short sheep-bitten grass.

A procession of travellers straggled ahead as far as the

eye could see. They were a mixed company; men carrying bundles, women carrying babies, donkeys carrying old women. A troup of minstrels trailed along weighed down by the instruments strapped to their backs, a harp, a lute, a drum, a set of bagpipes; they all looked equally weary though a little man who walked ahead cheered them on with a shrill tune on a reed whistle. Pedlars trudged with heavy packs; friars had bundles tied to their staves. A party of raffish men and women in shabby finery sang and giggled noisily. And among it all two showmen were urging on a hot and dejected performing bear.

The summit of the downs once passed, the land began gradually to fall away again, ridge succeeding ridge, to a blue and wooded line of distance.

Master Fetterlock halted Bayard and waited for his son who had hung behind with Hal to watch the unhappy bear. When they caught up he pointed to the expanse ahead. Lost in the shadows of the vale before them lay the town of Newbury.

Cecily's father and his hawks

Chapter 9

CECILY

THE way down the hill was easy and they covered it
quickly. Once more on the road they rejoined the
stream of traffic, heavier than ever now. But they did
not follow it for long. After a mile or so they turned off
across an open common.

A solitary horseman was riding towards them. Thomas
Fetterlock exclaimed under his breath.

'Hold yourself up, boy,' he said sharply to Nicholas.
'Keep your elbows in and mind your manners. It is
Master Bradshaw who rides to meet us.'

Nicholas felt that he was turning scarlet to the roots
of his hair. This tall man on a big black horse, with a
jewel in his hat, and a hooded hawk upon his fist, was
his future father-in-law. He wished that he dared stare
at him, but all he could take in of the man's personal

appearance was that he was broad and big, had fair hair, a prodigious nose rather like the hawk's, and a most merry smile.

The greeting between the two men was cordial. Then his father beckoned Nicholas forward. Evidently he was not expected to dismount, so he bared his head and bowed with all the dignity that he could muster. Master Bradshaw leaned across, and holding out a large and friendly hand, enveloped Nicholas's nervous one and shook it.

'So this is Master Nicholas,' he said briefly. 'He's well grown, big for his age. Do you hunt, boy? Can you fly a hawk?'

Trying hard not to stammer, Nicholas said that he had never had a hawk of his own. He had watched them, of course.

Master Bradshaw nodded casually. 'Oh, well, it is no matter. Cecily will teach you. She is crazed on hawks.'

He wheeled and fell into line between father and son. As the horses stepped forward, Nicholas found that his hand was shaking. Petronel felt it and started to prance. It did him good to steady her. When she was pacing evenly again he felt better. Cecily was crazed on hawks. She would teach him, would she? Somehow he did not think that he wanted to be taught by Cecily.

So long as they continued on the common they rode three abreast, and Nicholas listened in silence to the talk. They spoke of wool, and cloth, and prices, and the state of the market, but Master Bradshaw soon turned to sport. He described prodigious feats by his new hawk, a noble peregrine. Of course he should not fly her. He knew that. According to the law a peregrine falcon was not permitted to any below the rank of an earl. But

nowadays no one took any notice of these old rules.
His hounds, too, he described rapturously. He'd bred a
strain of hound which was the swiftest in the country,
and strong enough for a pair of them to tackle a stag at
bay. Had he told Master Fetterlock that he'd got some
red deer in the park now? They escaped sometimes on
to the downs, but that only made a fine course for the
hounds.

As he talked they approached a gate in a high fence,
each pale of which was sharpened to a point to make it
difficult to climb. This, Nicholas supposed, must be the
enclosed park of which his father had spoken. A wood-
man, apparently on the look-out, sprang forward to
open the gate and they rode through.

Inside the turf was soft and velvety, and big trees
spread their boughs, giving welcome pools of shade.

They had ridden only a little way when Petronel
went lame.

'She has a flint in her hoof,' Master Bradshaw said
to Nicholas. 'The flints on the common land are a
pest.'

His father told him to wait for Dickon. Dickon would
get it out if anyone could.

So, nothing loath, Nicholas waited. It took Dickon
some minutes to persuade the mare to submit to the
operation, and by the time that it was done the two men
were out of sight. The track was quite clear and easy to
follow, so Nicholas ordered Dickon to catch up his
master. Petronel must not be hurried, and he would
follow slowly with Hal. To Hal he confided that he was
so nervous that he felt sick. The longer it took them to
reach the house, the better he would be pleased.

It was peaceful in the park after the long strain of the
day, and they picked their way from one patch of

The girdle

shade to the next. Suddenly, as they passed under the spreading branches of a great oak, something descended from above – something long and shining and sinuous – and draped itself over the neck of Petronel before it slipped to the ground. The mare shied and danced on her hind legs. Nicholas's heart was in his mouth. But he regained control of her before she had gone very far, patting and reassuring her until he got her back in a wide circle to the oak where Hal, dismounted, stood looking up.

'What on earth was it?' demanded Nicholas. 'I thought that she would have me off this time.'

Hal extended his right hand, carefully, so as not to alarm the mare again. He was holding a long silver band.

'It's a girdle,' he said. 'A lady's girdle.'

'But where did it come from?' cried Nicholas in astonishment.

Hal lowered his voice. 'There's a maid in the tree,' he whispered.

Nicholas peered up into the branches. He could see a patch of cherry colour. It was true. There was someone up there. Petronel was now quiet, so he dismounted and approached the oak.

'Oh, please,' said a voice from above. 'I didn't mean to do it. I only wanted to peep, and then my girdle came undone.'

It was a girl, a little girl, younger than Nicholas. She was sitting on a cross bough, with her feet dangling and her skirt rumpled all round her.

'Who are you?' asked Nicholas. An idea had come to his mind, but he just couldn't believe it.

'I'm Cecily,' she said simply. 'I wanted to see you before you saw me, and I knew you'd come this way. So I got up into the tree. It's *our* tree, Walter's and mine. Walter is my brother. He made the hide in the tree, and it's quite easy to climb. But my mother will be dreadfully angry if she knows. She's told me so many times that I must give up climbing trees.'

The relief was so tremendous that Nicholas began to laugh. It was not only relief from the fright with Petronel, but also relief from all his dread. He had worked himself into a state of misery about meeting his betrothed. And here she was, not a fine lady nor a prim young mistress, but just a naughty little girl up a tree. As he laughed Cecily began to laugh too. Then Hal joined in, and the three of them laughed till they could scarcely stop.

'Hadn't you better come down?' suggested Nicholas at last.

'I can't,' she explained. 'I'm stuck. My dress is caught on a branch, and I can't move.'

There was only one thing to do. Hal had to hold both horses while Nicholas climbed the tree. It was easy enough to unhitch the dress and then, at Cecily's request, to 'turn the other way' while she got down.

When she was safely on the ground he was able to have a look at her. She was not, after all, so very small; in fact he guessed that she must be quite big for eleven. She was certainly not pretty. Her nose was turned up and bridged with freckles. Her fair hair, with a glint of gold in it, was parted in the middle and tied into two tight plaits. Her mouth was large, and when she smiled it was very large indeed. But the smile lit up her whole face, so that her small blue eyes shone and she radiated happiness. There was no question about it. She was, in his father's words, 'a good lively maid'.

'I don't know how you can climb trees in those clothes. It must be very dangerous,' he reproved her.

Cecily suddenly blushed right up to the roots of her fair hair.

'Well, you see, as a rule I don't –' She hesitated a moment. Then she went on in a confiding tone – 'It's a great secret, but when I climb trees with Walter I wear his tunic and hose. You won't tell?'

Nicholas shook with laughter again. This maid was not like any he had met. He promised to keep the secret. She looked anxiously at Hal. 'How about him?' she asked. 'Is he your servant? He won't tell, will he?'

Nicholas reassured her. Hal could always be trusted in anything.

She gathered up her skirts. 'Don't be too quick,' she begged. 'I'm so late that I'll get into the most terrible trouble. I've got to put on a new dress, a white one, to meet you. Do help me. If you have to change your clothes after your journey, be as slow as you can.'

Without waiting for an answer, she ran.

Nicholas stood and watched till she was out of sight among the trees. Well, whatever his betrothed might be, one fear, anyhow, was at rest. She certainly was not a little prig. He turned back to Hal.

'We won't mount again,' he said. 'We'll walk the rest of the way. That will give her more time.'

*

He had been in the house a couple of hours before they met again. Quite cheerfully he and Hal appeared at the door on foot. His father was watching anxiously to see what had become of him, but Petronel was a sufficient excuse. He was presented to Cecily's mother, a sweet delicate-looking dame, with Cecily's pale gold hair, but it was when he saw Master Bradshaw again that he realized whence she had her merry smile.

The house was very old – a rambling place built largely of timber with an upper storey projecting over the lower one and a deep thatched roof. Modern improvements had been added, such as chimneys and glass windows, but there was still a moat all round it and a fortified gatehouse, remaining from the days when it was a local stronghold.

The two fathers and his hostess were gathered in the hall, a fine roof-high room, hung with trophies of the chase and an ancient suit of mail belonging to Cecily's grandsire. He had to drink a cup of wine after his journey, which he quaffed at a gulp, believing it the manly thing to do. Tired and excited as he was, it went straight to his head, but his father helped him upstairs to their sleeping chamber, on the plea that the boy was weary and dazed after a long day in the saddle. He lay on the bed while his father himself pulled off his boots without even sending for Hal or Dickon. There was a pewter ewer and basin standing on a coffer, and when he had sluiced his face with cold water, he felt quite fresh again and able to change from his riding clothes into a doublet of blue edged with silver, with a deeper blue cote over it. The new hose, of finest cloth, were cut on the cross to fit his legs like a skin, and, coupled with the stiffness that beset him, made him feel like a jointed dummy.

In their absence the hall below had been prepared for a feast. The great table stood on a dais across the end, and in a gallery over the carved screens of the entrance passage some musicians sat, peeping down into the hall. Master Bradshaw was waiting for them with a small boy of round and angelic countenance, whom he presented as Robin, his second son. Nicholas did his best to talk to Robin, trying to remember what had interested him at Robin's age, but the child was tongue-tied and they relapsed into silence.

Suddenly Master Bradshaw exclaimed: 'Here they are,' and Nicholas turned round.

Mistress Bradshaw was descending the stairs, and behind her came Cecily, followed by Mistress Bradshaw's gentlewoman. It was such a different Cecily that Nicholas scarcely recognized her. She was dressed in a white gown sewn with tiny pearls, her plaits had vanished and her hair was almost covered by a stiff little white coif which strapped under her chin and made her look like a large solemn-faced baby. At the foot of the stairs her mother waited, took her by the hand, and led her forward.

'This is Cecily,' she said simply.

At the words Cecily looked straight at Nicholas and smiled, the same merry smile lighting her whole face. It was a friendly smile, intended, he knew, to refer to their last meeting, and she followed it by curtsies, first to his father and then to himself. Delighted, Nicholas half smiled back, then remembered his manners, and bowed deep.

'Go and kiss her, boy,' said Master Bradshaw heartily, behind him. In a panic of shyness Nicholas took another step forward. But there was no shyness about Cecily. As he approached she lifted her face and gave him a hearty kiss. He stayed beside her, thankful that it was all over, and grateful that she had helped him through it.

There followed the business of offering gifts, a ceremony which Nicholas found even more embarrassing than the meeting with Cecily. He had to do all the presentations. Hal, spruce in his russet doublet, stood behind him to hold the various presents which had been provided by his father. For Mistress Bradshaw there was a spoon and fork of crystal and silver; for Master Bradshaw a pen case of silver with a ring and chain to hang from his belt. And for Cecily – as

Presents for Cecily's father and mother

Nicholas saw again his offering for his betrothed, he gasped, and then struggled with an overwhelming desire to laugh – for Cecily he had brought a girdle, beautifully wrought of linked gold rings with a jewelled clasp. He did not dare look at her as he presented it. Behind him Hal was overcome with so severe a fit of choking that he had to leave the hall.

It was a critical moment but it passed safely. Supper followed. A chaplain said grace, and Nicholas found himself on a fine chair between Master Bradshaw and Cecily. The thought crossed his mind that this was the first time that he had been at the high table as a guest and not as a page. He noticed that Dickon was among the serving men, and Hal too. There was music from the gallery. He could distinguish a lute and a viol; he thought there was a harp as well. He had never before realized what a good idea it was to have music at meals; one did not have to talk. People went on putting food in front of him, and wine in his cup. He supposed that he ate and drank. But he could remember nothing about it all, except that he slept on a trestle bed made up beside his father's, that it had a feather mattress and that it was soft.

Next morning, to church

Chapter 10

THE COMFIT JAR

THE next day, to Nicholas's secret disgust, was Sunday, which meant getting up betimes and riding into Newbury for High Mass. Although the Bradshaws kept a chaplain to have daily Mass in their own chapel, on Sunday mornings they must attend the parish church like everybody else.

Nicholas was tired. After yesterday's long ride he did not relish hoisting himself into the saddle again. At Burford, he thought wearily, it was so easy just to run down the street, and Master Richard did not spin out the ceremonies as they did in this big town church, filled with burgesses and their ladies showing off their fine clothes, shopkeepers and craftsmen with their wives in stuff gowns, and the local lads crowded just inside the doors, blocking out all the air. There was some satisfaction in finding that the church was dedicated to

St Nicholas, his own patron saint. Perhaps that was a good omen, a sign that his betrothal was not such a bad thing after all.

Everybody else seemed fresh and cheerful in the morning air: Mistress Bradshaw sweet and smiling, anxious to know whether her guests had slept well; the two fathers cracking their private jokes together; Cecily prancing on Meadowsweet, her white pony. Even little Robin had found his tongue. Nicholas felt that he was the only dull one, except for Hal, who had lain all the night long on the floor at the foot of his young master's bed, and who was, he admitted in a sepulchral whisper, as stiff as a corpse on a gibbet.

After the High Mass they went to the Town Butts, where all the men and boys of the parish had gathered

Weekly practice at the targets

to shoot with the longbow. This weekly practice at the targets on Sundays was a law of the land, a law which, in spite of a few chronic grumblers, was universally popular. It was a very good-natured crowd that gathered along the boundary line, sitting cross-legged on the ground, waiting their turn with the bows and arrows, and munching the bread and cheese which they had brought to eat between morning and afternoon church. Each arrow that quivered in the centre of the target produced cheers, and every wide shot was acclaimed with hoots and catcalls. Nicholas was amazed at the standard of the shooting. Even the boys, who by law were allowed a shorter range, valiantly twanged their bow-strings at the official 220 yards target. Nicholas exchanged glances with Hal. This was very different from the butts at Burford. How would they acquit themselves here?

But Master Bradshaw set their minds at rest.

'No need to wait in that rabble,' he said as he beckoned them away. 'There are butts in the park at Beechampton, so we can practise our archery in comfort. Some of us are very pretty shots, we would have you know. What say you, daughter?'

Cecily tossed back her hood and laughed. Might they not go and look at the fair-ground? she begged. Many of the booths were already up. But her father shook his head. It was too hot. They would have more than enough of the Fair when the time came.

The rest of the day passed quietly. Dinner was eaten in the hall, with all the retainers seated at a trestle table in the body of the hall, and all the family on the dais. Robin and his two little sisters from the nursery appeared, as well as a flaxen-haired little girl of about Cecily's age, the daughter of a kinsman, who lived with them and shared Cecily's lessons. She was tongue-tied and prim, and tidy, exactly what Nicholas had feared that his betrothed might be.

After dinner they went to the butts in the park and watched the servants and the farm hands at their practice. They would not, Cecily announced, be required to go to Newbury again for Evensong, as, though they had to support the parish church for Sunday Mass, they might hear Vespers in their private chapel.

When the servants had shot their quivers-full and departed, Nicholas stuck half a dozen arrows into the ground in front of him, grasped a bow, and fired all six in quick succession. All

Nicholas stringing Cecily's long yew bow

but one landed somewhere on the target. Rather pleased with himself, he looked round to see if Cecily was watching. To his astonishment she was struggling to string a long springy yew bow which was much too hard for her. Nicholas offered her the one he had been using, but she said that she preferred her own, if he would string it for her. Then she selected an arrow, took careful aim, and placed it neatly in the very centre of the bull's-eye.

Nicholas was struck dumb. He handed her another arrow, but she shook her head.

'It was a chance,' she said modestly. 'My brother Walter always bade me stop if I had a lucky shot. I might never do it again. Walter is wonderful with the longbow. He has a crossbow too; he shoots rabbits with it. I've had enough of archery. Let's go and see the hawks.'

Nicholas remembered that Cecily was 'crazed on hawks', and how he had hated the idea that she should teach him. Now, oddly enough, he felt that it might be rather fun.

The hawks were all chained to their perches in the Mews, a building on the far side of the stable-yard. Mark, the falconer, an old bearded man who sat with a handsome hawk on his fist, feeding it with tit-bits of meat, looked up at them rather crossly. This was Master Bradshaw's noble peregrine, and she was not too friendly to strangers. But Cecily refused to take the hint and go away until she had shown Nicholas her own hawk, her little merlin, which she assured him was as tame as a kitten. Bidden by her, Nicholas stroked with a feather the back of the pretty little blue-grey bird, which, at her voice, came sidling along the perch. But he did not much care for the look in its eye, and he could well believe it when Cecily told him that in the air it was very fast and very fierce.

She took him round introducing each of the half-dozen hawks in turn. There were two large goshawks – they were really the most useful; a hobby, a fine cruel-looking bird with white throat and black moustache: the chaplain's sparrow-hawk; and a couple of hand-some kestrels for the servants (though, she whispered, they really weren't much good, except for rats and mice).

Nicholas looked wise so as not to give away his ig-norance, and studied closely the various objects hang-ing round the walls in order to remember them and their uses: *Jesses*, with bells, to strap to the hawks' legs; *Lures*, shaped like birds' wings which concealed pieces of raw meat to coax them back to their masters; hoods of soft leather, with gaily coloured plumes, beautifully shaped to cover the hawks' eyes. He would never have imagined, from seeing a hawk in the air, stooping on a partridge, or a hare, or a pigeon, that it was all such a complicated business. It was also a smelly one. The mews reeked of birds and raw meat, and he was glad to get outside again, and visit the fresh, sweet-smelling stables, where he could fondle Petronel without fear, and give her handfuls of fragrant hay.

When they had been the tour of the stables, they came out into the yard uncertain what to do next. It was very hot, so Cecily led the way to the herb garden

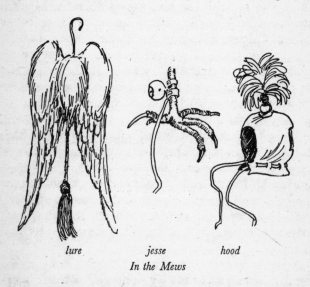

lure   *jesse*   *hood*
In the Mews

where they sat down on the grass in the shade. Cecily picked daisies and threaded them in a chain, while Nicholas chewed the ends of grasses, wondering idly why they had so many different flavours. It was cool and peaceful, and it took his mind back to the last time that he had lounged on the grass, the day of the dog fight. What a long time ago that seemed. He had not really been at peace since then. He laughed to himself as he remembered how he had begged Uncle John to take him to the Indies. He did not in the least want to go to the Indies now.

Hearing him laugh aloud, Cecily asked what he was laughing at. He told her about Uncle John, and about his ships and charts and his plan to sail across the ocean. Cecily was thrilled. She wished that Robin could hear it. Robin was crazed about ships and mariners and voyages of discovery. Nicholas really must tell Robin. She could not think where he could be; they had not seen him since they were at the butts.

Quite suddenly she scrambled to her feet. 'I will go and find him,' she declared. 'Do you wait here. I shall not be more than a Paternoster while.'

Before he could say a word she had vanished round the corner of the hedge.

Nicholas sighed. She was like a little darting fish, off in a flash. He wished that she had not gone to find Robin. He did not want to tell Robin anything, and was feeling a pang of conscience that he had chattered about Uncle John's business. After all, it was supposed to be a secret.

However, to his relief, in a very few minutes, possibly time to say ten Paternosters but no more, she reappeared alone.

'I cannot find him,' she said with a sigh. 'They told me that he has gone walking with my father. Do you like comfits?'

She flopped on to the grass again, and placed in front of him a jar of sweetmeats.

Nicholas stared. He recognized the jar at once. It was

a white jar decorated with a blue fleur-de-lis – almost exactly the same as the one he had seen in his mother's bower.

'Where did you get that?' he exclaimed.

Cecily lifted the lid and poked about inside. 'It was a gift,' she said, 'from a gentleman who is a friend of my father's – a Lombard. What do you like best – cherries or ginger or a sugar plum?'

Nicholas disregarded the question. 'It was Messer Antonio Bari,' he said almost triumphantly.

Cecily paused, a sugar plum half-way to her mouth. 'How did you know?' she said. 'He brought it only a few days ago.'

It was quite simple to explain. When they compared notes it became clear that the Lombard, with his guards and his packhorses, had lodged at Beechampton Manor the night after he left Burford. Cecily liked Messer Antonio. He came quite often, for he bought cloth from her father to send to Italy. He was kind, and he always brought her presents. But there was another Lombard, a horrible ugly man, dressed all in black.

Nicholas nodded. 'I know him. I call him Toadface.'

'A very good name,' she approved. 'I tell you he is a cruel man. I had a kitten and it scratched him. It was only a baby kitten, but he picked it up and wrung its neck – and then threw it down dead.' She shuddered at the remembrance. 'Ugh! I *hate* him.'

A sudden thought struck Nicholas.

'Did they both come this time?' he asked. 'The day you got the sweetmeats, I mean.'

Cecily considered a moment. 'Messer Antonio came alone – at least just with the escort men. Your "Toadface" must have arrived later, for they both left together in the morning.'

Nicholas felt quite excited. He knew the reason for that late arrival. He had seen the man with his own eyes at Leach's barn. 'It is a funny thing,' he said. 'You cannot get away from the Lombards. They are everywhere.' He was quoting what Uncle John had said to him, and Giles the shepherd too. Now he was finding for himself that it was true.

Cecily nodded thoughtfully. 'You are right,' she said. 'Shall I tell you a strange thing that happened? After that man had killed my kitten I had bad dreams every night and my father took me away with him. We went to stay with my grandmother. She lives in the New Forest.'

'I know,' said Nicholas smiling, 'near Beaulieu Abbey.'

'Quite near,' agreed Cecily. 'It is deep in the Forest. But even there I met the Lombards.'

Nicholas stared. Surely she must be making it up. 'The Lombards? *These* Lombards?'

She nodded again. 'Not Messer Antonio, but the other: Toad-face, as you call him.'

'But what was he doing there? Had he come to visit your father?'

'No, my father did not see him. I was out with my cousins. He was riding; just riding through the Forest, at the end of a string of packhorses.'

'I suppose he was going to Southampton,' Nicholas hazarded. 'The Lombard galleys lie at Southampton.'

'It was *miles* from Southampton,' retorted Cecily quite crossly. 'No one could possibly go to Southampton that way. I told my father about it, but he only said that the comings and goings of Lombards were a mystery too great for him to solve.' She leaned towards Nicholas and lowered her voice. 'Do you know,' she whispered, 'I *hate* that horrible man. I believe that he is the devil come to earth. I'd like to throw some holy water at him just to hear if it would sizzle.'

But Nicholas's mind was busy with more practical matters. 'Are you sure he was alone?' he persisted. 'Messer Antonio was not with him?'

She shook her head.

'There *was* a man with him, but it was not Messer Antonio. It was a strange man. He was riding a piebald horse.'

Nicholas almost shouted at her. 'A piebald horse? A black and white one? Are you certain?'

'Quite certain,' she answered. 'I always wish when I see a piebald horse. We all wished – my cousins too.' She stopped as she saw Nicholas's face. 'Why, is there anything the matter?'

Nicholas answered slowly and solemnly.

'I rather think that there is,' he said.

There and then, sitting on the grass, he told her the whole story, beginning with the coming of the Lombards, and the dog fight, and the lashes across Hal's face. Then he told her what Giles had said, about the ugly things going on, and how Uncle John had insisted that by lending money, the Lombards were getting all the country into their power. Finally, he told her about Leach and his mysterious barn and his secret meetings with the Lombards. He was sorely tempted to mention his own father, that he, too, was in debt to them, but he managed to resist the temptation.

But even without this additional touch, Cecily was thrilled.

'Have you told your father all this?' she asked when Nicholas had finished.

Nicholas shook his head. 'He will not hearken. He

likes the Lombards, and will hear no word against them. I must know more before I can speak again. If only I could find out why Leach should be riding with Toad-face in the New Forest, all those miles away from home.'

But though they discussed the whole business over and over again, to that question there seemed to be no answer. Nevertheless upon one thing they were agreed. The truth must be discovered. Toad-face and Leach and, if needs be, Messer Antonio himself, must be shown up and brought to justice.

How all this was to be done they had not yet decided when the chapel bell rang to call them to Vespers, and there was no chance of more talk that night.

The tenters, where the cloth was dried and stretched

Chapter 11

CLOTH

NOR was there time in the morning for talk.

Master Bradshaw's guests were to be taken on a tour of his business. They must be shown, from start to finish, the workings and wonders of the clothier's trade. They would begin by riding round the neighbourhood, where the cottage women took the raw wool and spun it into yarn, and then go on to Newbury to see the yarn woven into cloth on Master Bradshaw's most up-to-date looms.

So quite early they set out on horseback. Cecily came with them astride her white pony, her full skirt draped like Saracen trousers. Her father seemed to take her everywhere, as though she were a boy, instead of leaving her to the lady-like tasks of her mother's bower. Hal was there too. With Dickon and the Bradshaws' groom, he was to mind the horses.

They were too big a party to ride together, so Cecily was sent on with Master Fetterlock to lead the way while her father followed with Nicholas.

Thus left alone with his future father-in-law, Nicholas was engulfed in shyness, but Master Bradshaw soon put him at his ease.

'Well, my master,' he began cheerfully. 'If you are to wed a clothier's daughter, it is fitting that you should learn something of the clothier's trade. That should not be hard when you have a wool-man for your father. I suppose you've handled a fleece in the raw or are you afraid of soiling your hands?'

Nicholas was indignant. He explained that the shepherd's cot was his foster home. He could shear a sheep as neatly as anyone, except of course Giles himself.

Master Bradshaw smiled. 'I ask your pardon,' he said. 'I had not realized that I was talking to an expert. But do you know what happens to a fleece after you have shorn it? Doubtless most of your clip goes to Calais, or do you give any to be spun locally?'

Nicholas answered easily enough. He was at home with the workings of his trade. Most of the wool went to Calais, but dealers from Witney took some for blankets and of course some Burford folk bought from the clip to make their own clothes. Quite a lot of them had looms.

'*Burel*,' said Master Bradshaw briefly. 'That is our name for coarse home-woven cloth. It is warm and hard-wearing enough, but very different from the cloth you will see today. Of course, before it is ready for the loom the wool has to be washed and carded and spun. Have you ever tried to card a lump of rough wool, boy?'

'I have tried,' said Nicholas ruefully, frowning at the memory. 'Meg, the shepherd's wife, showed me. But I took all the skin off my hands.'

'Of course you did,' laughed Master Bradshaw. 'The cards are sharp; the very word tells you that, if you remember your Latin – *carduus*, a thistle. All my carding,

She managed to ply her spindle

and spinning, is done by village women. My packers take the wool round to the cottages, and collect the yarn a week or two later. We are coming to a cottage now, where the good wife is one of my best spinsters. She can make a thread as fine as a cobweb.'

They were riding down a sloping bridle path towards a group of thatched cottages, poor places by Burford standards, built mostly of clay daub, with scarcely a brick or a stone between them, but fresh with new whitewash and gay with roses and gilliflowers.

Outside the first of these cottages Cecily had dismounted and stood talking to a woman who, with a distaff tucked into her belt and a swaddled babe under her arm, was nevertheless managing to ply her spindle with her free hand.

'How now, mistress?' cried Master Bradshaw as they rode up. 'I have been telling the young master here that you can out-spin a spider. Put down that son of yours – or is it a daughter? No matter. Fetch your cards. I would have you show him how you turn a sliver of fleece wool into a fine thread before he can say his morning prayer.'

Delighted the woman dumped the infant on the ground from where Cecily promptly picked it up and vanishing into the low doorway, soon reappeared carrying the tools of her trade.

A spiked card like a hair brush

'See there, my boy,' said Master Bradshaw, holding out his hand to take one of the spikey cards. 'Small wonder that you skinned your hands. Do you feel those points now. They are made of thorns stuck into a leather back. Would you like to try again? No? Well, I would not blame you. Here, mistress, here is your card. Now let us see how you use it.'

With a spiked card, like a hairbrush, in each hand, the woman obediently took a piece of rough fleece, and tore it and teased it and combed it between them until it was almost as smooth as a lock of hair. Then she rolled it into a sliver, and laying the cards aside tied it lightly to the distaff.

'It looks as easy as patting butter,' remarked Master Bradshaw. 'And now do you watch her fingers. She will draw a length of wool out from the distaff and affix it to the spindle.'

'I can spin,' Nicholas broke in eagerly. 'I love spinning. I can spin a whole spool without breaking the thread.' He stopped suddenly and, blushing, looked round him. He had forgotten that his father was there.

Thomas Fetterlock was laughing. 'Methinks I should have had a daughter instead of a son,' he said. 'But I agree with Nicholas. Spinning is a wonderful business. The woman who first thought of it was the world's greatest inventor. It seems to me like a miracle when

I remember that every separate thread in every piece of cloth has been spun by some woman's hands.'

They left the good wife at last, still dropping and catching her spindle and winding up the thread with a sort of rhythm that matched the lullaby which she hummed to her protesting child. Master Bradshaw said that they must linger no more. They had wasted enough time if they were also to see the looms and the dyers and the fullers before they went home to dinner.

They approached the town along flat marshy land beside the river Kennet. Ahead of them lay a cluster of new buildings, barns and sheds and cottages, flanking a stretch of mown grass on which stood rows of wooden racks and screens, like neatly-arranged gallows, many of them hung with lengths of cloth. These were the tenters, Master Bradshaw explained, where the cloth was dried and stretched. There seemed to be a chain of these drying grounds, reaching right across the water-meadows, each with its lines of tenter racks. They did not all belong to him, Master Bradshaw explained, as he noticed Nicholas's wandering eye. There were Master Winchcomb's grounds, and Master Dolman's, and several others as well. The clothiers shared the marsh between them, since everyone needed river water and tenter fields.

Though Master Bradshaw's horse was accustomed to see lengths of cloth hung up to dry, Petronel regarded them as something exciting, and Nicholas had all that he could do to coax her to go quietly. He was glad when, beside a new long barn, men came running out to take the horses' heads, and it was time to dismount.

One end of the building was walled off as a counting-house, with a counter-board and stools and samples of cloth hanging from pegs on the wall. Peeping through a big door alongside Nicholas could see that the rest of the building was a warehouse with rolls and bales of cloth stacked upon shelves.

Master Bradshaw led the way into the counting house, drew up a stool for Master Fetterlock, and the two men were soon deep in some problem which involved much searching among leather-bound ledgers. He turned to Cecily.

'We have some business to consider,' he said. 'It will not take us long, but if you like you may take Nicholas to see the weaving. Leave the horses here, and run along the alley to Peterkin's. We will join you later.'

Her eyes sparkling with delight at being allowed to do the honours, Cecily darted out into the sunshine, and waited for Nicholas who stayed to receive his father's nod of dismissal. She glanced at Hal, standing with the other men beside the tethered horses.

'Would he like to come?' she asked Nicholas softly, and when Nicholas said Yes she beckoned. Walking between the two boys she guided them past the warehouse into a close of trim cottages. From each one came a familiar thump and clatter, which Nicholas recognized as the rattle of a working loom. Her father had built the cottages, Cecily explained proudly, so that his weavers should live near the drying grounds.

From one close of cottages they passed into another, and then along an alleyway, at the end of which stood a larger house, two-storied, built with heavy oak timbers and a bright red-tiled roof.

'This is where Peterkin lives,' Cecily announced as she tapped on the door. 'He is the master weaver. He makes a piece of cloth for the others to copy, and he's always inventing new weaves. My father says that the other clothiers would give their eyes to get him; but however much money they offer he will not go – not even to Jack of Newbury.'

'Who's Jack of Newbury?' asked Nicholas.

'Master Winchcomb, another clothier,' said Cecily airily. 'His tenter grounds are next along the marsh. He always wants to go one better than anybody. My mother says he was just an apprentice who married his master's widow. His name was really Smallwood, but he altered it to Winchcomb because he was born there and it sounds grander. I would not like to alter my name, would you?'

'Well, you are going to,' said Nicholas pointedly. Cecily blushed red as both boys began to laugh. She said hastily that no one seemed to have heard them, and banged again on the door.

Small wonder that they could not be heard, thought Nicholas as he listened to the steady pounding of a loom at work on the upper floor.

The door was opened at last by an old woman who smiled at Cecily and bade them enter. Inside was a large kitchen divided by a line of stout oak posts which helped to support the weight of the upper room. Near the wide hearth stood a wheel at which apparently the woman had been working. Nicholas crossed to look at it. He thought it was a new sort of spinning wheel, but Cecily shook her head.

'It is but for winding the yarn on to bobbins for the loom,' she declared. 'Peterkin is upstairs. Do hasten, or we shall have no time.' She led the way up narrow twisting stairs.

Almost the whole of the big attic above was taken up by the loom, the uprights of which were fastened to the cross beams of the roof. On the working stool sat a man throwing a shuttle unerringly backwards and forwards through a maze of lines and threads, while his feet trod the pedals. Two boy apprentices hovered round, fitted new bobbins into shuttles, eased the roll of woven cloth, or, at his word, pulled one or another of the harness cords.

As soon as he saw Cecily and the boys he stopped work, and in the sudden uncanny silence they found that they were shouting. Cecily explained that her father had sent them. He wished the young master to see the loom at work. The weaver, a spare, grizzled

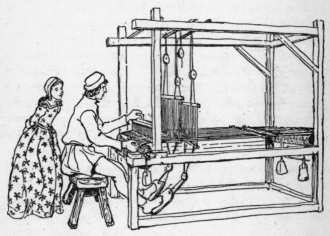

A man throwing a shuttle . . . through a maze of lines and threads

little man, looked from one to the other and smiled. From the expression of his face Nicholas was certain that the betrothal was no secret to him. But he was willing enough to show off his craft and began straightaway to explain the working of the loom.

He was weaving a piece of fine undyed cloth. The warp threads, which were to run through the whole length of the cloth, were stretched along the loom from one big roller to another. The farther roller, steadied by heavy weights, fed out the warp as required, while the near one rolled up the finished cloth. A harness of vertical threads and wooden battens, controlled by the pedals, separated the lines of the warp so that the shuttle containing the weft thread on its bobbin could be thrown from side to side to form the breadth of the cloth. How anyone could possibly throw a shuttle with his right hand through so narrow a space, catch it and throw it back again with the left, and at the same time use the rod which beat the cloth firmly together was an amazement to Nicholas.

Cecily, however, was all agog to try. It seemed as though this was the first time she had paid a free visit to her father's looms. Peterkin smiled indulgently and made room for her on his stool. But, alas, her feet could not reach the pedals and the beautiful pear-wood shuttle would not go anywhere that she wanted. After she had made three unsuccessful attempts she gave it up, scrambled down from the seat and ran to look out of the dormer window.

'Oh, come and see,' she cried. 'It looks on to the highway. There are crowds of people going into the town.'

Nicholas and Hal peeped over her shoulder. The window faced down an alley on to the main road. A stream of country folk passed along taking their wares to the fair-ground, farmers with loaded carts, good wives prodding sulky donkeys, and every form of livestock, pigs, calves, lambs and a flock of angry geese refusing to be driven from the stream at the side of the road.

It was fun to watch, but they had only been there a moment when voices on the stairs announced the arrival of Master Bradshaw and Master Fetterlock. The boys dutifully turned back to the room, leaving Cecily at the window. Now that the master had come, the weaver began to show off his loom in good earnest. The shuttle flew from side to side, the pedals and the battens thumped and clattered. Peterkin was told to demonstrate the wonders of the elaborate harness suspended from the roof, by which the warp threads could be lifted in groups so as to make a fancy weave. This was something in advance of Newbury's usual plain wool cloth. It could even be possible, Master Bradshaw boasted proudly, to form a pattern after the fashion of the Italian damasks.

*

They had said good-bye to Peterkin and were back in the open air before it was discovered that Cecily was missing. The old woman from the house said that she had left ten minutes ago, alone.

'She has run back to the counting-house,' said her father. 'Silly maid, not to tell us that she was going.'

But the old woman shook her head. The young mistress had gone the other way. She had run out into the road and turned towards the town.

Master Bradshaw frowned. 'Into the road?' he repeated. 'What did she want in the road? And where is she now?'

That question nobody could answer. Everyone hurried out on to the highway and stood in the stream of traffic, but without seeing a sign of Cecily.

'She has gone to look at the fair-ground, I'll be bound,' declared Master Bradshaw angrily. 'She is besotted with the thought of the Fair. By heaven, she shall be punished for this.'

Nicholas offered to go and seek her, but her father shook his head. 'You would not know where to look in a strange town. We will go back to the horses and I will send the men.'

But before the servants could mount Cecily appeared, hot and out of breath. She had been running. Her kerchief was crooked and her coif on the back of her head. She halted in front of her angry parent, obviously expecting trouble.

'A pox on you, wench. Where have you been?' stormed Master Bradshaw. 'Were you ill? No? What then? You *saw* something? What did you see? Some japes or trumpery, on my life. Are you a wanton maid to run wild at a fair? Home you go, mistress, and home you shall stay. I've half a mind that it shall be on bread and water. You have seen all the Fair that you shall see this year. That shall be your punishment. You shall not go to the Fair at all.'

Cecily's lip trembled, but she did not cry. For one moment she looked towards Nicholas. There was something in her glance that he could not understand, some message that she was trying to convey. Then her father began again.

'Get you into the counting-house and wait there till we come. There is still much to see, and I would not have the young master's day spoiled because of a silly wench. Stay you inside, and do not dare to move.'

He stalked away with Master Fetterlock, followed reluctantly by Nicholas.

There was certainly still much to see, but Nicholas found it difficult to keep his mind upon it. He stood gazing into vats of inky liquid, all looking very much alike whether they were made of woad, to give blue and greens and purples, or of madder for crimson red and the ever popular 'murrey', and he listened to Master Bradshaw's description of the dyeing of the cloth. But his thoughts were with Cecily. It bothered him to try and imagine what she had wanted to say to him.

Dyeing the cloth

After the dyeworks they went to see the fulling mill, where the cloth was steeped in water and pounded with a sort of smooth clay called fuller's earth which left it clean and soft and pliable, with all its wool felted together. After fulling it was hooked on to the tenters to be stretched and dried. Then the nap was raised with teazles, the thistly head of the common blue teazle plants which he had often seen growing without really knowing why people grew them. Even now he was not very clear about it, for after the nap had been raised by teazles, the cloth was then taken to the shearman, who laid it on a bench and shaved it all smooth again with the long blades of his gigantic scissors.

The Shearman shaved it smooth

But by this time Nicholas could no longer take anything in. He had more than his fill of knowledge. He
wanted to get back to Cecily, and he wanted his dinner.

*

On the way home he had to ride between his father and
Master Bradshaw, while Cecily, still in disgrace, followed by herself with the servants behind her. But as
the way became narrower, he managed to drop back to
her side.

'Why did you do it?' he reproached her in a low
voice. 'It has spoiled everything.'

'I saw them from the window,' hissed Cecily in an
urgent whisper. 'I tried to make you understand but
you took no notice.'

'I did not hear you. *Who* did you see?'

'The Lombards of course; both of them. I thought

I couldn't be mistaken, but I had to make sure, so I followed them. They are at the White Hart Inn.'

Nicholas was speechless. So this was why she had run away and got herself into so much trouble. But he would not let her off lightly.

'It was stupid of you,' he said crossly. 'Now you will not be able to come to the Fair.'

Cecily tossed her head. 'Oh yes, I shall. I may get a whipping, but my father will not hold me from the Fair. You see!'

Nicholas frowned. If it had been his own case he would have preferred a beating, but somehow he did not like the idea of Cecily being whipped.

The party reshuffled after entering the park gate, and Nicholas found himself riding with Master Bradshaw.

His host turned to him. 'Your father has pleaded with me,' he said. 'I have decided not to keep the maid from the Fair. It would spoil everyone's pleasure. I shall give her a whipping instead.'

Nicholas almost laughed. How well Cecily knew her father. But he had made up his mind what to do. 'Sir,' he said with great deliberation, 'will your worshipful mastership of your goodness whip me in her stead?'

Master Bradshaw looked at him with open mouth. 'What!' he cried. 'A whipping boy? Has the little minx so bewitched you that you would take her punishment for her?' Then he burst out laughing. 'In faith, we cannot beat a guest. I do not know if she has put you up to this, boy, but if she has she deserves to win.' He turned in his saddle and beckoned to Cecily. 'Come here, you witch. Your gallant has set you free. We will say no more about it.'

At the Fair

Chapter 12

THE FAIR

CECILY was not the only person who had seen the Lombards. As Nicholas dismounted, Hal, who stood waiting to take Petronel, signed that he had something to say. Nicholas followed him into the stable-yard.

'I've seen the two foreigners,' he whispered. 'The one that hit me, and his lord. I thought you might like to know.'

'Where did you see them?' asked Nicholas quickly.

Hal grinned. 'Well, sir, while you and the masters were going round the dyeing, Dickon and me ran up and had a look at the fair-ground. Master Bradshaw's man said we'd have plenty o' time; his mastership was a bit long-winded when he showed people round. So we just legged it. That's where I saw them – looking about – just as we were.'

Nicholas nodded his thanks. The bell had rung for dinner and there was no time for more. But after dinner he and Cecily met in the garden. She had really very little to report except that she had noticed the two Lombards from the window and had followed until she saw them vanish into the White Hart. The question was, what were they doing in Newbury at all, when they were supposed to have left for Southampton?

But it was not possible to go on talking because Robin found them and stuck closely to Nicholas, asking questions about Nicholas's Uncle John, and his ships and his charts, and the wonderful voyage that he was planning. Cecily had told him about it, and he couldn't rest until he heard more.

Nicholas was annoyed. He remembered guiltily that he had chattered about it to Cecily, and he bitterly regretted it. Quite crossly he told Robin that it was a secret and that he must never repeat it to anyone; and afterwards he gave Cecily a good talking to, as if the fault were hers and not his own. He explained that Uncle John had been specially anxious that the Lombards should not hear of his plan. Cecily promised solemnly that she would not breathe it to a soul, and she would see that Robin did not breathe it either.

The rest of the day was spent with family games, which stopped any more talk. First Nicholas was honoured by being included with the grown-ups in a match on the bowling green, cool and shady under its clipped yew hedge. Next Master Bradshaw insisted on teaching them a game called Golfe which consisted of knocking a ball into holes in the ground with sticks weighted by strange iron knobs. Nicholas had never played the game before, and his father said that he had not seen it in England, though he had come across it in the Low Countries. Master Bradshaw related that in Scotland, so he was told, it was so popular that the

A game called Golfe

King had forbidden it altogether because it made the people neglect their archery.

The afternoon ended with a romping game of Hoodman Blind to please the children, in which everyone got very hot and dirty. Afterwards, when Nicholas and his father were alone in their bed-chamber preparing themselves for supper, he remembered the Lombards.

'Did you know, sir,' he began a little timidly, 'that the Lombards are in Newbury?'

Master Fetterlock paused in the act of combing his hair. He was obviously startled. 'Lombards! What Lombards?'

'Master Bari and the other,' said Nicholas, satisfied that he had made an impression.

'How do you know? Have you seen them?' asked his father quickly.

Nicholas replied that Cecily had seen them, and so had Hal. Cecily said that they often stayed in this house.

At that the storm broke. 'Cecily. Hal.' His father

broke out sharply. 'What interest have they in the Lombards? What have you been saying? Does this mean that you have been talking about those matters of mine which I told you were not to be discussed?'

Hastily Nicholas denied that he had mentioned his father's affairs. He offered rather a lame explanation about the jar of sweetments and the killing of the kitten. But Master Fetterlock paid scant attention. He was angry.

'I warn you, my son, that clacking tongues will be your undoing. You prattle and prate for all the world like a woman, and with Hal, too, a servant I would have you remember. As for Mistress Cecily, you would be wise to start as you mean to go on, and permit no gossiping. Men in our position cannot put our wives in the ducking-stool, more's the pity. A dip in cold water is the best cure for a scolding tongue. But we can beat them. I admit that I've not beaten your mother since the early days, but she learned easily, and she knows better than to let me hear her clacking, if clack she must – and I suppose that every woman is a gossip.'

He paused a minute, as though bent on his own recollections. Then he took Nicholas by the neck of his doublet and gave him a little shake. 'But in heaven's name, boy, learn to control your own speech. A prating woman is bad enough, but a man with a clacking tongue is a despicable object and a menace to all who put their trust in him.'

He turned back to the business of his toilet while Nicholas struggled to steady himself. His conscience told him that his father was right. He had allowed his tongue to run away with him, and if he had not actually betrayed his father's secret, he had certainly given away his uncle's.

After a few minutes Master Fetterlock relented a little.

'About the Lombards,' he said. 'A mart such as Newbury Fair is exactly where you would expect to find them. There is nothing strange about it. Doubtless they have been to Southampton and come back again. It is but a day's ride. Your story about the kitten I grant you is not a pretty one. But you must remember that they are Italians, and in Italy tempers are hot.'

Nicholas felt that on the whole he had got off pretty lightly. When his father spoke about the Lombards he made everything sound so normal and above board that it seemed as if they had been making a fuss about nothing. Yet that was not how Giles looked at it, or Uncle John either, and he had not even dared to mention the mystery about Leach.

It was difficult to know what to say to Cecily. He did not want to admit to her that he had been taken to task by his father. However, as luck would have it, he rode abroad all next day alone with his father and Master Bradshaw on another rather dull tour of Master Bradshaw's business, and the morning following that was the opening of the Fair.

*

Nicholas, as a budding merchant, started early with his father and Master Bradshaw. Cecily was to come later with the children, attended by Mistress Lovejoy, her mother's gentlewoman, and a couple of serving men.

Newbury town, when they rode into it, looked as though it were Sunday. All the shops were shuttered, and bellmen paraded the streets proclaiming that the Fair had begun and that until it closed no one might offer goods for sale except within its gates. Nicholas's eyes opened wide. There was no fuss like this about a fair in Burford.

Master Bradshaw, seeing his face, laughed. 'That's just the way of the world, boy,' he chuckled. 'This is the New Fair, founded by the late king, the fourth Edward. The Crown takes two-thirds of the tolls, so you may be sure that no one is allowed to miss it. Now the old Newbury Fair, on St Bartholomew's day, has been going for hundreds of years, but the profits are for the poor at the Hospital, so you won't find the King's officers worrying about that one.'

The town was full of people in their best clothes, all heading in one direction, and long before they sighted the entrance to the fair-ground, Nicholas could hear the noise, the cries of vendors and the blare of bagpipes and horns and drums, and every sort of music.

They dismounted at a tavern and the men led away the horses. The fair-ground was fenced round with spiked palings laced with branches of holly and thorn, and the entrance gate was guarded by officials wearing the King's badge. Master Bradshaw paid the toll for all of them, and they passed in.

Nicholas looked round in amazement. Compared with this the little fairs in the Burford street were not fairs at all. Under a cloudless sky the scene blazed with colour. Tents and booths, hung with cloths of every hue, were arranged in streets, each street occupied by a particular trade, with the banners of their craft guilds erected across the entrance; clothiers, wool merchants, mercers, haberdashers in one alley; in another all the leather workers, saddlers, harness-makers, the cordwainers who made shoes and the cobblers who repaired them. In another part all the shopkeepers of the town were dealing with their everyday custom, since at fair-tide a man must buy even his daily loaf inside the toll gate.

Master Bradshaw was soon held talking by one merchant after another, so Thomas Fetterlock took his son by the arm.

'Come,' he said, 'till our host is less busy, we will look at the sights for ourselves.'

To Nicholas's joy he called Hal, and the three of them pushed their way through the crowd, ignoring alike the merchants who draped their wares across their counters, the apprentices who bawled at all and sundry, and the pedlars with trays of ribbons and gaudy knickknacks who waylaid them at every turn.

At the centre of the Fair, the hub from which the streets radiated, stood a big tent above which fluttered the arms of England and the banner of Newbury town. King's officers stood by the entrance, and the crowd, instead of pushing as it did elsewhere, gaped from a respectful distance.

'That's the Court of Pie Powder,' said Master Fetterlock as they passed, 'where the Justices try all cases connected with the Fair.'

'What has it got to do with Pies?' inquired Nicholas.

'Nothing,' said his father tersely. 'Pie Powder is really Pieds Poudrés, the Court of Dusty Feet. It is called that, I suppose, because it deals with wayfarers and travellers, everybody from a merchant to a vagabond, who is a stranger to the town. It tries all disputes at once and finishes with them, and, what with thieves and cheats and disputes about bargains, it is kept busy. Come along, boy. What are you gaping at?'

Nicholas had fixed his eyes on that part of the Fair which lay beyond the big tent. That was where all the music was coming from, and there seemed to be all sorts of exciting things going on. He could see people walking on stilts and brightly-coloured bladders tossed into the air. There were puppet shows too and see-saws and swings and he could hear the bang of the pole tilted at the Quintain, and the roars of laughter from the crowd.

His father suddenly realized what he was looking at and laughed.

'Oh, set your heart at rest. You'll find plenty of japes and mummeries over there later. Bide a while, though. I've other things to show you first.'

He led them into an alley where the crowds were more orderly. A few country folk passed, awestruck, down the middle, but most, noting the sturdy watch-men with shining halberds, hastily turned the other way. This was the quarter of the goldsmiths, where the rich foreign traders had their stalls. Here strolled the prosperous merchants with their ladies, peering at the finely wrought jewels, carved ivories and sandalwood, books beautifully bound with golden clasps, goblets of exquisite glass, and wonderful silks and damasks.

'You must buy a fairing,' said Master Fetterlock. 'Look about you, son, and choose something for your mother, and something for your Mistress Cecily, too.'

This was a weighty business and required much thought. In the end Nicholas chose for Mistress Fetter-lock a set of silken tassels of different colours to mark the places in her prayer book. For Cecily he picked a tiny pomander ball in filigree silver, gilded on the out-side. It was intended to hold sweet-scented spices and there was a silver ring at the top by which it would hang from the girdle – a dainty toy, said Master Fetter-lock with a smile, pleasing for a child and fitting for a woman. Nicholas had chosen well.

When they joined Master Bradshaw again, Nicholas had to submit to a lecture on the different varieties of cloth displayed on the clothiers' stalls, and to finger them till he could tell with his eyes shut a smooth broadcloth from a ribbed kersey, and a kersey from a

The bear dancing to pipe and tabor

rough frieze. This duty done they repaired to the tavern to dine.

All the alehouses of Newbury had set up their bushes on gaudy poles decorated with streamers in the section of the Fair set aside for Victuallers. Master Fetterlock said that they would drink wine today, and Master Bradshaw must be their guest. He led the way to a bench under the sign of the Swan with the Two Nicks, the mark of the Vintners Company, where they ate large slabs of pasty washed down by wine of Gascony.

Scarcely had they finished their meal when Mistress

Lovejoy arrived with Cecily and the children, and the rest of the day was given up to merrymaking. Cecily and Robin wanted to see everything, and their father supplied money from his well-filled purse. There were jugglers and tumblers, Morris dancers with bells on their shoes, cheap jacks bawling their goods, and quacks who offered cures for every known disease. There were booths where it cost a penny to see a puppet show, and there, surrounded by an admiring crowd, was the same sad performing bear, solemnly dancing to pipe and tabor. As a contrast to all this, a friar on an upturned cask was preaching to as many as would listen, exhorting them to go and be shriven before the coming feast of Corpus Christi.

After a while Nicholas and Hal drifted away from the others. Hal wanted to go to the part of the Fair where everyone could test their skill, either at leaping or at casting the weight, or wrestling, or a bout with the quarterstaff. At home in Burford he was cock of the walk, for his uncle, Nash the barber, who had fought in the recent wars, had passed on all his old soldier's tricks. Here in a bigger town it might be a different story; but all the same he wanted to try.

He started modestly enough against lads of his own age, but he could cast the lead farther than any of them, and leap farther too. He twirled the quarterstaff round his head with such a mighty swing that the crowd fell back in alarm, and in the wrestling he threw two opponents both bigger than himself. At last the master of the wrestling booth, thinking that it was time that this young cockerel learned a lesson, challenged him, and when Hal was rash enough to accept, threw him with such a right good will that Nicholas feared that he must have broken a rib at least. But the wrestler knew that

Hal thrown in the wrestling booth

he would not gain customers by breaking ribs, and Hal got up slowly with nothing shattered except his pride. He limped away with Nicholas, pursued by the jeers and cat-calls of the lads of Newbury.

To give Hal time to recover Nicholas decided that he himself would hire a lance to tilt at the Quintain. The target hung from one end of a crossbar swivelled on an upright post. From the opposite arm of the crossbar hung a bag of sand. The game was to charge at the target and hit it a resounding blow, and then dodge the counter blow from the bag of sand, as it swung round. It was a game of skill calling for speed, but Nicholas was nimble on his feet and the Quintain was his particular fancy.

The boy ahead of him had been caught, greatly to the delight of the crowd, but Nicholas took careful aim. Eyeing the pitch, he counted his paces and started on the right foot, so that he should land with the left foot free to dodge. At his first attempt the sack missed him by a matter of inches, and enjoying the applause, he succeeded in repeating his success twice more which won him a rosette to put in his hat. He was more pleased still when he discovered that Cecily and the children had joined the crowd to watch him, and with a grand air he presented the rosette to Cecily. But a murmur from the crowd made him look round again.

Hal charging at the Quintain

Hal had followed him to the Quintain. Not to be beaten by his master, he was charging down the pitch with a gusto that made Nicholas hold his breath. The fool! He could not possibly check himself and dodge at that pace. Sure enough, as his lance smote the target, the sandbag swung round with terrific impetus and in another second Hal was sitting on the ground, holding his pate and wondering what had hit him.

The crowd roared with joy. Hal had asked for it, and he had got it. Nicholas laughed as loud as any, and Robin was bent double with glee.

'Oh, I am *stabbed* with laughter,' he cried. 'Will he do it again? Do ask him to do it again.'

Cecily stamped her foot angrily. 'Shame on you for a lot of heartless loons,' she rated. 'Do you not care if he is hurt?' She pushed her way through the crowd and rushed to Hal's side. Mistress Lovejoy followed her and examined the pigeon's egg fast rising on his head.

'Run to the apothecary,' she bade Cecily. 'Ask if he has a salve of hazel or of wintergreen to stay the swelling.'

'A frog cut open and laid on warm is what my mother taught me,' suggested one old dame, while another recommended the lard of sucking pig mixed with garlic. But before any of these fearsome remedies could be obtained, Cecily returned with a phial of liquid which the quack had assured her was the elixir of health, certain to cure all ills. Poured bodily over the bump it was at least cooling. Hal got to his feet, and soon he was sufficiently recovered to retire with the others to a gingerbread stall.

But though Hal had had his fill of excitement, there was still one thing that Nicholas hadn't done. Leaving them all watching yet another puppet show, he hired for himself a pair of stilts. He had walked on stilts at Burford fair and was rather proud of his skill. Lifted well above the heads of the crowd, it was a grand way to see everything. Greatly daring he ventured out of the fun fair into the alleyways of the mart. They were almost empty. Business was over for the day and the merchants were beginning to pack up their stalls. He stumped at quite a good pace down the street of the clothiers, up past the saddlers, and down again by the goldsmiths.

Suddenly he stopped, grasping the post of a guild sign to keep himself from falling. Ahead of him stood three men deep in conversation – his father between the two Lombards, Messer Antonio Bari and Toad-face.

Master Fetterlock was leaning against the corner of a booth. Even from so far away Nicholas could see that he looked grave and worried. The two Italians were talking and gesticulating at him, both at once; Toad-face with much shoulder-shrugging, Messer Antonio thumping one fist on the palm of the other hand as though to drive home some point.

Nicholas recovered his balance, turned, and made his way back to the others. He felt guilty, as though he had been eavesdropping. He was thankful that his father had not noticed him, but the old uneasy doubts had returned. If the Lombards were such good friends, why did his father look so troubled when he was with them?

He found the rest of the party weary and ready to go. Nicholas and Hal, with the serving men, escorted them back to the tavern where the horses were waiting. They all rode home together, but everyone was tired and there was little talk.

The Corpus Christi procession

Chapter 13

THE SURETY

THE second day of the Fair was the feast of Corpus
Christi, a Holy Day of the Church, when all good
people attended Mass and there was a great procession.

The Fair would not open until the procession was
over, and even then no buying or selling was allowed.
But a Holyday was a holiday, and all the country folk
flocked to the town prepared to enjoy themselves.

The family from Beechampton Manor formed quite
a little procession of its own as it rode down to the
High Mass. So great were the crowds that, though
Mistress Bradshaw and her gentlewoman were ushered
to seats inside the church, the rest of the party got no
nearer than the step outside the west door. From there
they could at least see the glimmer of the candles on the
altar and hear distantly the plain chant of the choir. The
church was much too small, Master Bradshaw whispered
to his guests. It was high time that they built a new one.

But when the Mass was over and the time came for the procession to form up, it was the people outside the church who had the best chance. Master Bradshaw quickly guided his party by a short cut to a place of vantage and deposited them on a raised pathway from which they would be able to see the whole column from the moment that it turned into the market place. Crowds surged all round, scurrying through narrow ways from the church to take up positions along the route.

Even before the cross-bearer appeared round the distant corner Nicholas could hear the choir, as it emerged from the church, chanting the great processional hymn, '*Lauda Sion*'. Behind the cross, their embroidered banners held high, followed the Trade Guilds of the town, the Bakers, the Grocers, the Tanners, and all the rest, with the various crafts of the Cloth Trade, weavers, fullers, dyers, shearmen, massed together at the end. Last of all came the great Company of the Clothiers, under whose emblem walked the merchants, wearing their rich fur-trimmed gowns and heavy gold chains. Cecily, at Nicholas's side, suddenly nudged him, to make sure that he noticed her father solemnly pacing among his fellows. This, then, was why he had left his family so abruptly.

Though Nicholas had taken part in processions at home ever since he was a toddler, only big enough to strew flowers on the ground, he had never seen one as fine as this. After the Trades came the religious Guilds and Brotherhoods, the Guild of the Holy Name, the Guild of St Catherine, the Hospice of St Bartholomew, each carrying an image of its patron saint, and leading a company of the old people, or the cripples or the orphans whom the guild supported.

The gaily coloured banners were still passing along

the street, moving from brilliant light into deep shade
and out again, when the choir and the clergy with the
golden canopy turned the corner and came into view.
The hymn changed and the cantors sang the opening

notes of the '*Pange Lingua*'. The first soaring line of the
familiar chant awoke echoes everywhere among the
crowd. Timidly at first a few people joined in; then,
gaining courage from each other, more and more in a
swelling unison till the very walls of the town seemed
to be singing. Then, gradually nearer, a new sound
approached – the tinkling of bells. As though a sickle
had swept along the street the crowd dropped to its
knees. The tide of voices ebbed as heads were bowed,
while the canopy beneath which the priest carried the
Blessed Sacrament passed slowly by. This climax over,
the people scrambled to their feet and, taking up the
chant again, fell into line at the tail of the procession.

> *Genitori, genitoque laus et jubilatio*
> To God the Father, God the Son
> Songs of praise and hymns of joy.

Nicholas threw back his head and let himself go. A
wave of emotion swept him along. The sun, now high
in the heavens, lit up the brightly-coloured figures

moving against the deep shadows of overhanging houses. He glanced at Cecily, who was walking a few steps ahead of him. Her merry twinkle was replaced by an expression of intense solemnity, and she was singing with all her heart. Suddenly Nicholas was conscious of great happiness. Praise and joy. Praise and joy. Life was certainly very good.

*

Early the next morning Nicholas and his father made their farewells. Master Bradshaw, Cecily and Robin rode part of the way with them, leaving them at almost the identical spot where Master Bradshaw had met them the day that they came.

As Nicholas swung Petronel round to wave good-bye, he reflected how different were his feelings now from those of a week ago. He liked all the Bradshaw family, and with Cecily he was firm friends. Everybody, he supposed, had to be married some day, unless they were priests or monks. That being so, he couldn't imagine anyone whom he would rather marry than Cecily. It had been arranged that before very long she was to come with her parents to Burford for a return visit, and he was actually looking forward to it.

It was with a light heart that he followed his father up the hill. The downs today were deserted, for Newbury Fair was not yet over. On the summit, where a long stretch of sheep-bitten grass lay ahead of them, Master Fetterlock set Bayard at a canter. Nicholas, pulling off his hat for the pleasure of feeling the wind through his hair, followed him. He would like to have shouted aloud for happiness.

As they came to the end of the down, Master Fetterlock slowed up and waited for Nicholas.

'You were right about the Lombards being in Newbury,' he observed casually, as their horses paced side by side. 'I met them at the Fair.'

Taken by surprise Nicholas almost blurted out that he had seen them together, but he thought better of it.

His father apparently had decided to take him into his confidence. 'We had weighty matters to discuss,' he said. 'Now, since you are my only son, and should anything happen to me my business would be yours, I have determined that you shall know as much as possible about it.' He looked at Nicholas and gave his short little laugh. 'Anyhow it seems that your eyes are bright, and if you are going to use them, I would have you understand what you see. Therefore, if there is anything in what I am going to tell you which is not clear to you, I desire you to ask me.'

He paused a minute to let his words sink in. Then as Nicholas murmured only a dutiful reply, he continued slowly and deliberately.

'First of all,' he said, 'you may as well know that I have undertaken to stand as surety with the Masters of the Staple for Messer Antonio Bari in the sum of five hundred pounds. Do you know what that means?'

Nicholas shook his head. He did not understand a word of it.

'Listen you carefully then. To stand surety is to offer a pledge of money that Messer Antonio, when he exports wool out of England, will not break certain laws of the Staple. If he should break them and be found out, I should have to forfeit five hundred pounds. Is that clear?'

Nicholas said Yes. But secretly he was appalled. Five hundred pounds was a fortune. He did some rapid calculations. Petronel had cost five pounds. Therefore this was the equal of a hundred Petronels.

Master Fetterlock, unaware of his son's arithmetic, continued his story.

'Maybe you wonder why I have consented to this,' he said. 'Five hundred pounds is a great sum, but it is quite safe. I shall never be called upon to pay it. You have, I know, listened to silly stories about the Lombards. Ignorant people talk of Italians as though they were all rogues and usurers. The Italian of good family is a fine and cultured gentleman. Messer Antonio, for instance, is agent for the noble Medici, the famous bankers. The modern world could not live without bankers. Even the King sometimes must needs borrow from them.'

Nicholas bit his lip. Uncle John had spoken about the King being in debt to the Lombards, but he realized in time that it would not do to say so.

'If the Lombards are bankers, can they be merchants as well?' he asked doubtfully.

'Of course they can,' said his father patiently. 'They bring Italian goods in their galleys, and carry back wool or cloth or tin or whatever we have to sell. They hold a special licence from the King to take wool to Italy, but, as you know, the Staple is very strict about any wool that goes out of this country. It will not allow foreigners to sell English wool in the markets of France or Flanders. There are Staple officers at the ports to see what wool the Italians ship, and make certain that it goes only to the Mediterranean.'

There was a pause. So Nicholas ventured a question.

'But why should Italians want to sell English wool in France? I should have thought that they wanted it to go to Italy.'

Master Fetterlock smiled. 'In this world, my son, everybody wants to make money. They could make a much bigger profit by selling quickly in a rich mart, than by wasting time on the journey to Italy. Remember that the galleys take six or seven months to get home. I am glad that you asked that question, for it helps me in what I want to explain.'

They were leaving the hills now, and for a time they had to ride in single file down a steep track. It was very hot, but at the bottom they found a pond where the horses could drink while they refreshed themselves from the leather water-bottles that they carried with them. Then Master Fetterlock took up his story again.

Water bottle

'I was telling you that it takes about seven months for the galleys to reach Italy. It is much quicker to send the wool all the way across Europe by packhorse. But before a Lombard can land his cargo in France to start the journey he has to find a member of the Staple who will pledge a large sum of money that the wool will not be sold in any mart north of the Alps.'

When he ceased speaking there was silence for so long that he turned to his son and asked him quite sharply what he was thinking.

Nicholas plucked up his courage.

'Did you *have* to pledge for Messer Antonio, sir,' he asked, wondering at his own boldness. 'I mean, could you have said *No* if you had wanted to?'

'What do you mean?' retorted his father hotly. 'Of a certainty I could have said *No*. I still have my free will. But I should have been a churl, and ill-advised as well. Messer Antonio is a good customer, and a very good friend. He has helped me out of many a difficulty, and I am deep in his debt to this day.'

Nicholas bit his lip to stop himself from crying out aloud. That last sentence had made it all quite plain. Uncle John had been right. The Lombards had lent money to his father. He was in their debt and had to do what they wanted. Nicholas had seen it for himself in that short moment at Newbury Fair.

Master Fetterlock, glancing at his face, seemed to read some of his thoughts.

'Set your heart at rest, my son; it is not as bad as it sounds. As I have said to you, Messer Antonio is a man of honour. But, mark you, Nicholas, you may mention this to no one. Do you understand? To no one at all. There must be no more prattling and gossiping. I will not hear another word of foolish clacking. I have told you all this because I believe that once you know the facts your own good sense will control your tongue. I am a merchant of the Staple. You have seen for yourself that such a position is a goodly one. Because of it you are to marry the daughter of a wealthy man. But remember, the betrothal is not yet binding. The contract has yet to be signed. What do you think would be the result if it were spread round that the house of Fetterlock was in debt to moneylenders?'

To this question Nicholas could give no answer. He

would have liked to tell his father about Cecily's meeting with Leach and the Lombard in the Forest, but he just lacked the courage to provoke again the charge of gossiping. So he held his peace. Soon they reached Faringdon and stayed to eat bread and cheese and drink cool ale. A merchant joined them on the road, a wool-man going to the Cotswolds to buy fleeces from the new clip. Nicholas rode in silence while the two men talked. He was trying to sort out all that his father had told him. It sounded rather frightening, but if his father said that it was all right he supposed that it must be. At last, tired of worrying, he put the whole business away from him and looked about him instead.

At Radcot they paused a while to watch a barge being loaded, but once across the Thames it began to feel like home. In the excitement of Newbury he'd almost forgotten the shearing and now there were signs of it everywhere. In every field there were newly-shorn sheep, and the way was quite busy with wool-men and packers and poor ragged labourers, thrown out of work as the land was turned from corn-growing to sheep-farming, and now trudging from shearing to shearing in hope of a job.

Dickon was enjoying a passage of loud jest and laughter with the plump wife of a burgess of Faringdon who was riding pillion behind her husband hoping to pick up odds and ends of wool cheap, to spin and weave for her family; so Nicholas beckoned to Hal to join him. Hal was in high spirits. His only fear was that some of the shearing would be over. But anyhow there would be the supper. They settled down to talk about the supper. Newbury was a thing of the past.

*

They reached home while the sun was still high and found Mistress Fetterlock with a good meal ready for them and eager to hear 'all about it'. But when supper and the talk was done, Nicholas was free. He decided, tired as he was, to run over to Giles's and hear about the shearing.

Dickon enjoying a jest with a passer-by

As soon as he started down the hill he realized that he was the centre of attention. Though the sun was setting, many of the shops had not yet pulled up their shutters. In the cool of the evening the owners were still leaning out across them enjoying a friendly gossip. As soon as he appeared conversation stopped. Some of the men wished him a 'Good evening young master'; others merely grinned and nudged. One woman called out for tidings of Newbury Fair, and when he stopped civilly to answer, the others all gathered round to listen. It was obvious that he and his betrothal had been discussed in every home in Burford.

It was the same at the shepherd's cot. But though Meg was all agog for news, he could put her off 'till tomorrow' and Giles was quite prepared to talk about sheep. They sat down outside in the growing dusk and Nicholas, at last, was again at peace.

Giles reported that the shearing was going well. Leach and his team of hired men had sorted the wool as it was cut, and most of it was graded and packed already. Almost the whole clip was good enough to go to Calais, and thirty sarplers were packed for Southampton, for the order of the Lombards. Giles spat with deliberation as he mentioned them. Then he glanced over his shoulder to make sure that they were alone.

'I am not happy about things, my master. Tomorrow I must see your worshipful father. Last week I caught one of the packers cutting the feet and legs off a wool fell – a whole sheepskin – and folding it in a sack to pass as clipped wool. He was a new fellow, one of Leach's men. So I opened another sarpler and found it bearded with fine wool on the top and stuffed with refuse underneath – and all sewn up as grand as you please with the best Arras canvas and thread, and the Fetterlock mark.'

'Did you tell Leach of it?' cried Nicholas.

'On my life I did. He sent the man about his business there and then. If I'd had my way he'd have gone before the justices and spent a day in the pillory, but Leach said that it was not for the good of our name to let such things be known. He is the packer. It is his business, so I had no more to say.'

Nicholas was thinking deeply. 'You say that the man

had stuffed the sack with a wool fell? Where did he get his wool fell? We don't kill sheep at the clip.'

Giles chuckled with appreciation. 'You are a bright one, sir. That is the very thing that I asked Leach. He said that he had an order for a pack of wool fells and he had gotten some out of his barn.'

'Then he *has* got wool in his barn,' cried Nicholas triumphantly.

'What he has in his barn is known only to the blessed saints,' returned the shepherd, 'but methinks it is time that others should know as well. Leach has traffic with the Lombards; we know that; and I do not trust the man.'

It was on the tip of Nicholas's tongue to mention that meeting between Leach and the Lombards in the New Forest but he controlled the impulse. 'You will tell my father all this?' he urged.

'Heaven be my witness he shall know in the forenoon,' vowed Giles fervently. 'Tonight he will be tired after his journey, I shall wait on him by eight of the clock.'

But in the morning Giles had no chance to tell his story. After Nicholas had gone to his bed a messenger arrived with a letter from the Mayor of the Staple. It was a worrying letter, Mistress Fetterlock told Nicholas later. As the sun rose, his father was in the saddle and away to Calais.

Nicholas could shear a sheep as neatly as anyone

Chapter 14

SHEARING

AFTER the first shock Giles took the news of his master's going very calmly. He asked Nicholas how long his father was to be away, and when Nicholas could not tell him he said no more. Master Fetterlock was often from home, in London or in Calais, and the Cotswold end of his business was designed to be run by the two servants in authority, the shepherd and the packer. The shearing had begun in his absence and it would be finished in his absence, that was all. If Giles was troubled by what was going round him, he must keep it to himself. To Nicholas, for the present, he said no more.

Nicholas, too, seemed to have reached a full stop. He was worried, and more certain than ever that there was mischief afoot, but he had been so scolded about discussing his father's affairs that he did not dare even to talk to Giles. So he settled down again as best he could to his ordinary routine.

True that there was the shearing. It was an understood thing that his lessons with Master Richard were only one half of his education; for the rest he was apprenticed to his father, and must spend a great deal of time learning his craft. So, much to the disgust of Fulk and the other boys, who were to be clerks and must stick to their books, Nicholas was free to spend long summer days out of doors. He was determined to make good his boast to Master Bradshaw, that he could shear a sheep as neatly as anyone. He got tired and sweaty and dirty, and the whole world seemed suffused with the smell of sheep; but there was always the river to plunge into, and the hard work took every troublesome thought out of his head.

The sheep-shearing supper put the final touch to his cure. This feast, held in the biggest barn, had never before taken place in the master's absence, but Master Fetterlock had left word that it was to go on as usual, and that, if he were not back in time, his place was to be filled by his son – tidings that threw Nicholas into a ferment of excitement.

The supper was always a tremendous affair, attended not only by all who worked among the Fetterlock flocks, but also by any connected, however remotely, with the Fetterlock household, which in effect could be stretched to include half the town. To cook all the food was beyond the power even of Mistress Fetterlock's resources. The town bakehouse was engaged. Great casks of ale and cider and perry were trundled down the hill. The stonewallers built a special screen in the corner of the meadow where a fire could be lighted, and the smith manufactured a spit twelve feet long on sturdy iron tripods. Here by ancient custom a sheep would be roasted whole, and the lads of the town would take it in turns to crank the spit, undaunted by the raging heat and the spluttering mutton fat that spat savagely as the carcass revolved.

As an old friend of the family Master Midwinter was invited to take a place at the table as Nicholas's guide and stay. Master Richard attended for a short time to bless the meats, and the ancients from the almshouses chanted a special Amen. There were constant relays of musicians, since every soul in the town who claimed to play an instrument used it as a pretext to be there.

Only one figure was noticeably absent. Master Midwinter remarked on it at once.

'Where is that lean-faced packer of yours?' he questioned Nicholas. 'There is your shepherd at one end of the high table. By rights the packer should face him at the other. What has become of your Master Leach?'

Nicholas could not say. Master Leach had been round the farm in the forenoon. He had even watched the fire being lighted to roast the sheep, so he must have known about the supper.

'Well, he can be spared,' returned Master Midwinter cheerfully. 'A more dismal ill-favoured master I never did see. He rides round the country looking as if he had come straight from a dirge. And yet by all telling he has little enough cause. His purse is well-lined. He has just bought a palfrey for his wife for a matter of twenty pounds. The fellow must have money to burn. Twenty pounds, I tell you – for a palfrey.'

He thumped the table so hard with his fist that Hal, who, with the other lads, was serving, thought that he was calling for more drink and refilled his mug to overflowing.

As meats were carved and more casks tapped the

A sheep roasted whole for the shearing supper

noise grew louder and louder. Mutton joints, with the roasted flesh torn from the bone, lay scattered about the tables in puddles of ale and gravy. Labourers, who commonly saw little of such fare, mopped at the mixture with hunks of bread. When the time came for Nicholas to make his speech, he had to clear a space where he could stand on the table to make himself heard. He had dreaded this speech, yet in the end it was quite easy. Everyone there had known him all his life, and the story of his new betrothal was food for their ribald jokes. He was shouted down with cheers and laughter and clapping when he had got no further than to bid them welcome in his father's name. So he gave it up and signed to the pipers to begin playing. The trestles were moved and, though everyone held on to their tankards, the boards were just emptied on to the ground, where the dogs fought for the remains. A space was cleared for dancing. Nicholas joined in one or two

Bagpipes and hurdy-gurdy

romping rounds, 'Gathering Peascods' and 'Sellinger's Round'. Then darkness fell; torches were lighted. The dances and songs grew wilder and wilder, and Master Midwinter whispered to Nicholas that he had best come home. The people would be happier without the master.

All the way into the town and up the hill they were pursued by the sound of rollicking voices and the shrill discordant wail of bagpipes and hurdy-gurdies. Even when Nicholas opened his bedroom window to cool his throbbing head he could hear it still, floating from far away over the moonlit roofs and chimneys. He wondered suddenly where his father was, while all this was going on? That question led to a second – and where, also, was Leach the packer?

*

Sellinger's Round

The answers to both questions turned up the next day. Mistress Fetterlock received a letter from her husband to announce that he had returned from Calais, but it was necessary for him to remain in London for a while. She informed Nicholas of this piece of news just as he was packing his satchel. A few minutes later, on his way to the parsonage, he encountered Master Midwinter dismounting from his horse beside the striped pole of the barber's shop.

'It seems that more than the sheep need shearing,' he called to Nicholas. 'My hair is like a haystack. I shall soon have love locks like your father's Lombard lord.' He waved a friendly hand, and reached for the latch of the door. Then he turned back again. 'I hear that your man Leach had his own shearing supper last night. Perchance our company was not good enough for him.'

Nicholas, who was hurrying down the hill, stopped dead and retraced his steps.

'What did you say, sir? His own supper? Where? Who was there?'

'I'faith, how can I tell who was there? He may have supped with the devil for all I know. My man Gregory rode to Westwell yesterday – his mother was ill; and when he came home around midnight there were lights in Leach's barn. He could see them from afar off. He wondered at it since he thought that certainly Leach must be at the supper here.' He nodded, and turned again towards the barber's. 'Well, we did not miss him. How's your head, boy? A trifle queasy, I'll be bound.'

Giles, when Nicholas questioned him about Leach's supper, knew nothing of it. He growled that if Leach had a supper he must have had it alone. But Giles was certainly suffering from the effects of last night and was in no mood for gossip.

*

Now that the excitement of the shearing was over life settled into a dull routine. Master Richard expected Nicholas to make up for lost time, and kept him long hours at his books. Very little else happened. The customary midsummer fair on St John's feast, judged by the standards of Newbury, seemed little more than a glorified market day, but it served to break the monotony. Mistress Fetterlock, also, disturbed the peace by insisting that Nicholas must write a letter to Cecily. She knew of a messenger going that way and the chance must not be missed.

For hours Nicholas sat in misery at his father's counter, scratching his nose with the end of his quill. When he appealed to Master Richard for help, the priest replied with a smile that love letters were outside his province, and Nicholas should follow the guidance of his heart. But Nicholas's heart offered no suggestions. At last, in despair, he submitted to his mother's control, and wrote at her dictation a letter based on a scribe's collection of model letters. It was full of fine phrases and began by addressing Cecily as his 'Worshipful mistress and most sweet cousin' ('cousin', he was told, being a useful term which could cover any tie). It commended her piously to the care of the blessed saints, told her that he took no pleasure in life until he might be with her again, and that he was her true lover and humble servant.

He grinned to himself as he scattered sand over the ink, remembering Cecily up a tree, Cecily running away to track the Lombards, Cecily stamping her foot at them at the Fair. He sealed the letter with his father's seal – the merchant's mark so despised by Mistress Fetterlock – and then tried to forget it as quickly as possible.

The reply came in less than a fortnight, written in a round childish hand. He had not known for certain that Cecily could write. After all many girls were not taught anything but the domestic arts. But flowery as the letter was, he recognized a touch of the real Cecily about it. She called Nicholas her 'well-beloved Valentine' and told him that if only he were satisfied with her she would be 'the merriest maiden alive'. He laughed aloud at that. Of a truth he was very well satisfied.

But he had not yet finished with his letter-writing. One evening Giles took him aside.

'You are a scholar, young master,' he began. 'Could you make a letter for me to your worshipful father?'

Nicholas stared at him. 'Has anything happened that is new?' he cried.

Giles shook his head. 'It is just that Leach is sending away the wool for Calais. Since I found the bearded sarplers I have done all in my power to delay it. I have discovered reason after reason why it could not go, hoping that the master would come back. But now Leach will wait no longer. He is the packer and I cannot stop him. But I shall sleep better o' nights when your father has been told. I am no scholar, Master Nicholas, and I would not trust this matter to a scribe.'

That was true. It would never do to bring a public letter-writer into it.

'I could write the letter,' said Nicholas. 'But how could we send it? My mother's messenger left yesterday. There will not be another this week.'

'I have thought of that,' replied the shepherd. 'There

is a man who rides regularly for the Lord Abbot of Gloucester. He is courting my niece, and he will surely call at the barber's tomorrow on his way to London.'

Nicholas sighed. There seemed to be no help for it. And if the letter was to go in the morning there was no time to spare. Giles would have to tell him what to say, so he took the shepherd home with him, praying that somehow they would be able to elude his mother's eye. His prayer was answered, for in the town they met Mistress Fetterlock on her way to Vespers, with her primer, her rosary, and, as usual, Bel tucked away under her sleeve. Nicholas sighed with relief. His mother always lingered over her devotions. They would be undisturbed for an hour at least.

The letter itself was not nearly so difficult as the one to Cecily had been. He knew how to address his father; he had been properly taught. And what he had to say was not difficult either. When he had finished his composition he read it over to Giles.

To my worshipful master Thomas Fetterlock Merchant of the Staple, at London in Mart Lane be this delivered.

Right honourable and worshipful father. In the most humble wise I recommend me unto you, whom I beseech Almighty God to preserve in prosperous health and heart's comfort, desiring of you your daily blessing.

Sir, if it pleaseth you to know, your servant Giles commends him to you and hath prayed me tell you that he hath opened diverse sarplers of your Cots wool the which were packed under the hand of Simon Leach your packer and men of his trust. Giles hath found some of these sarplers sorely bearded with refuse, also one with wool fells feigned like good clip. The sarplers have set forth for Calais and he could in no wise hinder them.

Wherefore I humbly beseech you to let me know your pleasure how that you would have matters ordered as shall be for your worship and profit. No more, good father, but Almighty Jesu have you in His blessed keeping. Written at Burford on St Mary Magdalen's day. Anno Hen. VII 8°.

By your own Son,

NICHOLAS FETTERLOCK.

Giles was open-mouthed with admiration, and Nicholas himself felt that he had done well. He folded the letter, kindled a taper with his father's tinder-box, and sealed it with his father's seal. Then he gave it to Giles.

Well, it was done. He wondered if his father would answer it. He counted on his fingers; it would be six days at the very least before he could hear, and then only if his father sent a messenger immediately.

But the answer was more prompt than even he dreamed. On the evening of the fifth day his father arrived home.

*

Coming in to supper in the belief that, as was the recent custom, he would sup with his mother in her bower, it was a shock to find both parents already seated in the dining parlour. Nicholas was red with embarrassment as he made his obedience, but his father did not refer to any business. Throughout the meal he chatted of Calais and London, and the news of the town from each. Nicholas began to wonder if the messenger from Gloucester had been faithless after all. But at the end of supper, as he toyed with his goblet of wine, he smiled at Nicholas.

'You write an excellent letter, my son,' he remarked pleasantly.

'Letter,' said his wife sharply. 'What letter? I did not know that the boy had written to you.'

'A letter of business,' Master Fetterlock told her quietly, 'just from one merchant to another. The matter in it must wait until the morrow. Ay-de-mi, but I'm weary. Wife, with your leave, I'll to my bed.'

Though Nicholas was up early, his father was earlier still, and had somehow caused Giles to be fetched to the counting-house, even at that hour. Nicholas could hear their voices as he passed the door. It was an effort to hold himself in patience for the summons which he knew was bound to come, but actually Giles had left some time before his father called him.

Master Fetterlock, spectacles on his nose, was seated at his counter, which was almost covered by open ledgers.

'Well, my son,' he said. 'It seems that we have much to say to each other. I have told you that your letter pleased me. It was an excellent letter for a boy of your years. You may sit down. There is some deep mystery here, and I would fain solve it.'

He pushed back the books, tilted his spectacles over his forehead and, leaning his folded arms on the table, looked at Nicholas.

'I suppose you are on tenterhooks to know why I went so suddenly away. It is a long story but I will make it brief. I received a summons from the Staple, from the Mayor himself, that I should wait on him immediately at Calais. There were grave matters to answer. Sarplers of my wool, listed as finest Cotswold, had been found in the mart at Bruges half full of rubbish.'

Nicholas nodded gravely. It was what Giles had feared would happen.

'This is no surprise to you, of course,' his father went on. 'I have spoken long with Giles. It was great ill fortune that I did not see him before I left. But it must have been going on for some time. The new wool could not have reached Bruges yet. That means that it is more than the work of some dishonest labourer, and we must get to the bottom of it. Now, look you here. Giles has given me an account of all the fine wool which he has supplied for packing. It is all writ down.'

He pushed over one of the open ledgers and pointed to the neat columns of entries.

'We will say, to make it easy, that there was enough wool for fifty sarplers. Very well. I have written it in my book that fifty sarplers have been dispatched in one direction or another. So far so good. But if some of those sarplers have been bearded with rubbish, there must be a considerable amount of good wool which is missing. Where has that wool gone? That is what we must discover.'

There was a moment's silence. Then Nicholas plucked up his courage. 'Have you asked Master Leach?' he inquired.

His father smiled. 'Of course it is obvious to suspect Leach. But, my son, there may be more in this than we have yet seen; and it might be wiser not to give him warning until we know all.'

'Sir,' said Nicholas. 'There is a matter which I would fain tell you, but I fear that you may chide me again.'

His father frowned. 'I will not chide you. Tell me what you know. Does it concern Leach?'

Nicholas nodded. It concerned Leach and the Lombards. He described how they had asked the way to Leach's house, how he had seen the Lombard at Leach's barn and, last of all, how Cecily had seen Leach in the New Forest.

His father caught him up quickly. 'In the Forest,' he

exclaimed. 'Now of a truth that is strange. And they had packhorses, you say. Clearly they were going to Southampton.' He brushed aside Cecily's word that they were miles from Southampton. That was of no count. They were riding by some devious way, so that they should not be noticed, which made it all the more suspicious. He pushed back his stool and paced up and down deep in thought. At last he stopped and looked directly at Nicholas.

'I have rebuked you for your tomfoolery, boy, but I will admit that I may have been hasty. Messer Antonio is an honest gentleman; yet his secretary may be a knave. Well – prepare yourself for a journey. Tomorrow we ride for Southampton.'

The Mediterranean galley

Chapter 15

BY CHANCE AT WINCHESTER

THIS was news indeed. Nicholas spent the rest of the day in a whirl of excitement. This time he was to travel as his father's clerk, and he wore attached to his girdle not only an ample purse, but also a pair of neatly-hinged tablets, with wax surface, on which it would be his duty to write with a stylo, and keep records as his father ordered.

They followed the same route as last time. They would pass through Newbury, and Dickon was sent ahead with a message to Master Bradshaw begging that they might lie at Beechampton Manor that night.

So he was to see Cecily again even sooner than he had expected. Nicholas looked pleased, but his father issued a warning. Nothing must be said about the object of their journey. Nicholas could truthfully say that he was going to Southampton to learn his trade. Although certainly Cecily's story about Leach was the direct cause of their going, it would not do to mention it yet. While the troubles with the Staple lasted, the less that was said to anybody the better.

A pair of neatly-hinged tablets

When they had left Burford well behind them, Master Fetterlock began to explain what he hoped to do at Southampton. His purpose was to visit the Customs House. Every bale of wool which passed through the port was entered in the Customs ledgers, and a tax paid upon it before it was allowed to go to the ship. The Customs officers would know exactly how many bales the Lombards had taken on board and as he knew how many he had sold to them, it would be easy to check up. If Leach had delivered to them the stolen wool, it would be at Southampton that there would be a record of it.

Nicholas was thrilled. This was a real adventure; and might prove to be the solution of all the trouble and mystery. As for not telling Cecily, it did not worry him at all. Perhaps by the time they returned everything would be discovered, and there would be nothing left to hide.

As it happened there was no chance to talk to her, even had he wished to do so. At Faringdon they were delayed by a thunderstorm, and they arrived at Beechampton so late that the children had already gone to bed. Cecily was allowed to stay up in order to eat supper at the same table as her betrothed, but before the meal was finished she was told to say good night and Nicholas was left to play backgammon with his elders. The morning was wet, so she could not ride with them, but only wave good-bye from the shelter of the porch.

Newbury in the rain looked dull and dreary, very different from the day of the Fair, and though after a few miles the clouds lifted and the sun came out, the roads were a quagmire, deep with ruts and sticky with clay. At the summit of a long hill Bayard lost a shoe, and Nicholas had to share Dickon's horse, so that his father could ride Petronel. But when they reached a smithy, there were other travellers in the same plight, and they had to wait their turn. They strolled round the village, a poor primitive place where all the cottages were hardly more than hovels, with the old-fashioned smoke-traps in the roof instead of chimneys. A woman, for a penny, gave them a good meal of barley bread and sour cheese, washed down with rather strong goat's milk. Now, said Master Fetterlock with a smile, Nicholas would see why a traveller should always carry his own drinking horn and spoon.

By the time they were on their way again it was past noon, and it was decided that they should sleep the night at Winchester. There was a fine up-to-date inn there, the George, and as it was but twenty miles farther to Southampton, they could ride that short distance in the morning.

Winchester was a great city. The streets were crowded and the air seemed full of the sound of bells. They reached the George Inn, a well-built house with a fine painted sign of St George dispatching a very savage dragon, handed their reins to an ostler, and their saddle-bags to Dickon, with orders to have an eye on the horses and the luggage. Master Fetterlock beckoned Nicholas to follow him. They would be just in time for Vespers.

'A traveller should always carry drinking horn and spoon'

The first sight of the cathedral took Nicholas's breath away. He had never known so fine a church. Already it was almost dark inside, except for the distant glimmer of candles in the choir where monks were chanting the office, and for the little twinkling lamps that hung before the altars in the chantry chapels. But as his eyes grew accustomed to the dimness he could make out the pale masses of soaring columns in the vast height of the new nave.

Their prayers finished, Master Fetterlock whispered that they must go. It was too dark to see anything, and they would be the better for a meal. Nicholas was only too ready. He was so hungry that to sup seemed the only thing that mattered.

A delicious smell of roasted meats greeted him as he

followed his father into the hall of the inn. There were long trestle tables set round the sides where travellers of a more humble class sat on benches, cutting their meats on wooden trenchers, or tearing them with their fingers. Some produced food from their own packs, others supped simply with horns of ale, and broken loaves of bread. Torches stuck in holders gave a flaring smoky light. The noise was deafening and the floor slippery with trodden rushes and rejected food.

Through this confusion Master Fetterlock led the way to a door at the far end. They entered a dining parlour, a quiet decorous room where half a dozen merchants sat at a board spread with a linen cloth and ate from pewter platters, with bowls and napkins and all the furnishings of polite society. There was plenty of room at the middle of the table, for all the merchants were grouped at one end except for a solitary figure leaning back in a tall chair at the other. The candles on pricket stands close behind the chair lighted a profile which Nicholas could not mistake. It was Messer Antonio Bari.

If either the Lombard or Thomas Fetterlock felt half the dismay that seized Nicholas, they succeeded in concealing it. With an exclamation of pleasure, Messer Antonio pushed back his chair, and advanced with hand outstretched. It was indeed a fortunate meeting, he declared. He was just lamenting his loneliness, and wishing for some good friends to bear him company. He banged the table and demanded service for his guests – insisting that it was his turn to offer hospitality. Most certainly they must sup with him.

Even the shock of the meeting could not destroy Nicholas's appetite, and he devoured two courses of the excellent venison which Messer Antonio declared must

Messer Antonio pushed back his chair

surely have come from the royal deer in the New
Forest. But as the meal progressed it began to dawn on
him that all was not so easy as it seemed on the surface.
There was a restraint in the atmosphere, and he realized
that the two men were taking each other's measure,
like combatants in the lists. Messer Antonio wanted to

know what Master Fetterlock was doing in Winchester, and before long he inquired outright. Thomas Fetterlock replied truthfully that he had business in Southampton, and Nicholas fancied that the Lombard quickly raised his eyes and as quickly dropped them again. But the smile returned to his face, and he leaned forward to refill his guests' cups with the sweet Gascon wine which he had ordered.

'Indeed?' he said courteously. 'I thought that all your Staple merchandise went from the port of London or from Sandwich. Those thirty sarplers, so excellently packed, which you were good enough to purvey to me, have all been cleared by the Customs more than a week since. You need have no anxiety on that score.'

Master Fetterlock replied smoothly that, of course, he had no anxiety. Then in his turn he asked a question.

'You are alone?' he inquired. 'It is unusual to see you without your secretary.'

The Lombard shrugged his shoulders. 'Yes, he is away, I know not where, on some business of his own.' He turned to Nicholas. 'Will this be your first visit to Southampton, my young friend? I remember when I was a boy, how overwhelmed I was by the sight of all the ships in the harbour of Genoa. The first glimpse of a great port is a wonderful experience. Upon my word I think I must give myself the pleasure of riding with you tomorrow.'

Master Fetterlock intervened. 'We could not dream of imposing on your mastership,' he said firmly. 'You are a busy man, and we also have much to fill our time.'

The Lombard smiled his lazy smile. 'It would be no imposition. I should take pleasure in showing your son the sights.'

Thomas Fetterlock frowned. Obviously to have

Messer Antonio at his heels would be fatal to his inquiries.

'Nicholas must learn the duties of his calling,' he said stiffly. 'There will be no time for sightseeing.'

Nicholas, watching, was certain this time that the Lombard's eye glinted with a sudden cold light. But the lids dropped again and his tone was as suave as ever.

'Going in search of knowledge, eh? Well, treat her carefully when you find her, my boy. Knowledge is an uncertain jade. Just when you think that you have caught her, you see her laughing at you from afar. I am sorry that you will not see my galley, with your father's bales stowed neatly in the forward castle. But she has gone. She pulled out of port this morning.'

He glanced from one to the other, as though to note the effect of his words. Nicholas saw that, while his father's face showed nothing, the hand resting on his lap stiffened suddenly.

'You have been prompt, sir,' he observed in an even voice.

The Lombard flicked his fingers. 'We had no reason to delay,' he said, 'now that your mastership has made things easy for us with the Staple. Of course we did not dream that we should have the honour of a visit of inspection, or I should have bid my captain wait so that you might check the goods in comfort.' His lazy drawl quickened, and his lip lifted like a dog about to snarl. But he recovered himself, took a draught from his cup and turned the snarl into a laugh.

'However,' he smiled, 'the galley has gone, and by now she will be lying off the Isle of Wight to pick up water. It is odd, is it not, that the island water should keep fresh on shipboard longer than any other. Did you know that, young master?'

Nicholas said that he had heard of it. His Uncle John had said so.

Messer Antonio nodded several times. 'Of course; of course; your uncle the sea captain; I remember now. He knew the Island. He was an adventurous man. I heard a rumour that he planned to sail westward to find the Indies. I hope he is not greatly discontented that a Lombard should have got there first?'

Nicholas forgot his manners. 'What's that?' he cried. 'What did you say? A Lombard got there? To the Indies?'

Messer Antonio laughed at him. 'The young Englishman is dismayed,' he remarked. 'But it is true, my friend. The whole world knows it by now. Cristoforo Colombo has sailed to the west and reached land – either the Indies or some new lands near them. He sailed with Spanish ships and he returned to Spain more than three months since.' He brushed the crumbs from his gown and stood up. 'And now, my masters, I must bid you a very good night and go to my bed. I start on my way to London early in the morning. I trust that you will be successful in your mission and that you will find' – he paused, and a smile twitched the corners of his mouth – 'whatever you are searching for. Farewell, my boy. Another galley will call at Southampton in a few weeks' time, homeward bound from Flanders. Could you not ride again, and see that one? I should be happy to show you.'

*

When he had gone Nicholas and his father looked at one another. The other merchants had also withdrawn and they had the room to themselves.

'What did he mean?' asked Nicholas softly. 'He hoped that we would be successful in our search.'

His father nodded. 'I am glad you noticed that. Who said that we were searching for anything? *We* did not say so.'

'He would have come with us, if you had let him. And yet he said that he must ride to London.'

'He was taken unawares,' said Master Fetterlock. 'He knew not what to be at, but he desired to find out what it was that we were in search of. Ay de me,' he sighed deeply. 'I have trusted the man, and I would wish to trust him now, but I must grant that tonight he did not make me trustful.'

Nicholas drew a deep breath.

'Is it true, sir, about the Indies? Has Colombo really reached new land?'

'Yes, my son, I fear that it is true. In London it has been news for many weeks. I should have told you had not other matters filled my mind. Your uncle will find it hard tidings. I know not where he has gone. I have not seen him this long time since.'

'Uncle John said that the Lombards were in it,' Nicholas observed thoughtfully. 'He said that they were everywhere.' Then, noting a small frown on his father's brow, he changed the subject. 'Where shall we go tomorrow?' he inquired. 'I mean, will Southampton be any good now that we know the galley has gone?'

'That does not matter,' replied Master Fetterlock. 'The Customs will tell us all we need. Come, boy, we must to bed too. I shall be interested to see whether he lets us ride without him.'

But in the morning there was no sign of the Lombard. The innkeeper reported that he had paid his count, and left almost before the sun was up.

The City of Southampton

Chapter 16

CITY OF SHIPS

THE road from Winchester to Southampton was the busiest that Nicholas had ever known. There were sober English merchants riding with their clerks, and foreign merchants richly dressed in outlandish fashions. There were church men of every degree from a bishop in his purple, riding with a retinue of priests and clerks, to sandalled friars on foot, and palmers with cockleshells in their hats home from their journey to the shrine of St James at Campostella in Spain. There was a party of pilgrims, jabbering some foreign tongue, landed at the port to trudge their way along the downs to Canterbury. There was a great lord surrounded by gay courtiers, and a company of halberdiers, their term of duty at Southampton ended, singing as they marched, their armour shining in the sun. There were seamen, tanned by wind and weather, the prosperous ones riding nags, the others patched and shaggy and half-naked. And, threading their way through all the company, like the warp of a loom, there were packhorses, packhorses, and even more packhorses, some coming, some going, but always laden with bales of merchandise.

Nicholas would like to have ridden slowly, to take it all in, but his father was anxious to reach their destination. He knew the country well, and here and there he left the rutty road, taking circuitous bridlepaths, which seemed a long way round but which brought them back to the road again ahead of the company they had left.

At last, as they crossed an open common, a shining streak caught Nicholas's eye. It widened as they drew nearer until it lay before them, a broad sweep of water leading to the sea, with a great walled city jutting out to be lapped by its tides.

Nicholas gazed fascinated. He had never seen the sea, and as he faced into the wind he smelled it too, a tang that was new to him and which made him feel suddenly that he wanted to stand in the stirrups and shout.

They had to enter the town by the Bargate, a massive gatehouse with moat and drawbridge and portcullised archway, through which all traffic from the landward side reached this fortress of the sea. It was a long business for only one vehicle at a time could pass through, and every carter and trader had to pay a toll on the goods he carried. Nicholas fidgeted in the saddle. He wanted to go on to see what lay behind those forbidding walls which continued unbroken down the hill to the shore, where the water washed the base of the angle tower and flooded into the moat. He caught sight of some small boats riding at anchor, and the mastheads of larger vessels over the line of the battlements.

At last their turn came, and they crossed the drawbridge and clattered on the cobbles under the arch.

The Town Broker had his office in the gatehouse,

and in a stone passage, littered with sacks and bales, his underlings were busy collecting tolls. Master Fetterlock dismounted, threw his rein to his son and vanished into a dark inner doorway. Nicholas moved the horses out of the way and sat gazing at the scene before him.

It had been impossible to imagine that a bustling modern city lay within those ancient walls. A fine wide street stretched ahead from the Bargate. All the houses, three stories high, were gay with stripes of timber and whitewash, red roofs and painted signboards. The same procession of carts and packhorses continued down the centre of the road, while along the sides a mixed crowd of travellers and housewives with shopping baskets, gazed at the open counters. Along the inside of the walls stood market stalls, bright with fruit and vegetables, and, most wonderful of all, with glistening fish, fresh from the sea. Nicholas, who except for trout or perch from the Windrush, knew only salted fish, moved nearer to gaze on the clear shining colours, though the fish wife told him with a smile they were 'no but herrings and mackerel'.

On this side of the gate he was perfectly content to wait, though soon he found himself the centre of a circle of pedlars and beggars of every description, some offering for sale gee-gaws which reminded him of the fair, others, bandaged or on crutches, pressing near to exhibit their sores, while ragged urchins and mangy dogs somersaulted, pushed, and tumbled round the horses' legs. After a few minutes of this he was glad when his father, followed by the Town Broker, bareheaded and respectful, emerged from the gatehouse. At the sight of the Broker the crowd scattered, and as this potentate held Bayard for Master Fetterlock to mount, it was borne once more upon Nicholas that a merchant of the Staple was a very great man indeed.

But Thomas Fetterlock was ill content. The Broker's ledgers had helped not a whit, he said. They would ride on to the Wool House, where the bales were weighed and customs charged. They might have better fortune there.

For Nicholas, anyway, it was better fortune, for the Wool House lay at the extreme end of the town, just inside the seaward walls. It proved to be an ordinary

Nicholas and his father rode to the Wool House

storehouse, massively built of stone, and heavily buttressed. It was full of wool-packs and sheep skins, with porters unloading packhorses and other porters trundling bales on trolleys. Nicholas followed his father inside, leaving the horses tethered. He unfastened his tablets, and prepared his stylo, feeling that his duties as a clerk should surely begin here. But his father vanished again into an inner office, and after waiting idly for some minutes, the temptation to see what lay beyond the walls became too much for him. He discovered an open postern, ventured through it, and found himself actually upon the quay.

He had never seen a ship before, and the sight of the great hulls, built up with castles at the bow and the stern, just took his breath away. The pictures painted in the capital letters of one of Master Richard's books had provided all his fancies, and the reality was far more wonderful. Most of the vessels had one or two masts, but the biggest of all had three, with pennons flying and complicated rigging. There were sailors at the top doing something to the looped-up sails, and he wished that they would unfurl one of them, so that he could see if it really had arms emblazoned on it, like the picture in the book. Some of the smaller ships were just the same shape as the walnut-shell boats, their masts stuck in with sealing-wax, that Uncle John had made for him. He gazed wistfully at the little rowing boats that bobbed about everywhere. If only he dared just nod his head at one of the watermen who plied for hire.

His longing was written so plainly on his face when his father appeared, that his wish was gratified, and they sat for ten minutes in a creaking wherry and were rowed in and out among the great ships. The galleys had gone, the waterman informed them, unconsciously confirming Messer Antonio. They were quite different from other ships, with their long, pointed hulls and lines of oars. There would be more coming from Flanders shortly, on their way home to the south. It was a pity that the young master should miss them.

Back on dry land they made their way to a tavern for dinner.

As Nicholas's excitement died down, he remembered to inquire how his father had fared at the Wool House.

They were rowed in and out among the great ships

Master Fetterlock shook his head. 'It was no good,' he said gloomily. 'I had persuaded myself that at Southampton I should find the key to the mystery, and I have found nothing. I've seen the ledgers both at the toll gate, where the wool comes into the town, and at the Wool House, where it goes out; and I'm not a jot nearer the truth than I was. The Lombards bought thirty bales of my wool, and thirty bales, no more, no less, have passed through Southampton.' He cut a leg from the capon that had been placed before them, dipped it in the sauce and nibbled it thoughtfully.

'Couldn't the wool have gone from some other port?' Nicholas suggested.

His father shook his head. 'The Lombard galleys call only at Southampton or at Sandwich, and Sandwich is too far away. It looks, my son, as though you had started us on a wild goose chase, with your stories of Leach and the Lombards.'

Nicholas said no more. They rode back to Winchester almost in silence, and in heavy rain. The curfew sounded as they entered the town. Doors opened and hands stretched out to extinguish the lanterns which hung on every house. The streets became suddenly pitch dark. The cathedral rang the Gabriel bell, for everyone to say his evening prayer. Nicholas began an Ave but failed to reach the end of it. He was thankful to drink a mug of mulled ale and go shivering to bed.

*

The rain had stopped the next day for the return journey to Newbury. His father said no more of the great wool mystery, and Nicholas knew better than to start the subject. He longed to get back to Beechampton Manor. Though he was not permitted to mention the Lombards to Cecily, he was bearing the tidings that Colombo had reached the Indies. He could imagine the excitement with which Robin would receive that news.

Yet, somehow, even their reception at Beechampton fell a little flat. Master Bradshaw was out and did not return until supper time. Robin was a-bed. He had been naughty and his father had beaten him and locked him upstairs. Cecily, for some unknown reason, was kept closely to her embroidery frame and called back to her mother's side if she tried to leave it. Only Mistress Bradshaw was her sweet, gentle self. She took both the travellers into her bower, provided Master Fetterlock with a goblet of home-made wine and a book of romances, and Nicholas with some skeins of wool to wind for her tapestry. Then apparently fearing that the entertainment was somehow lacking, she produced a pack of French playing cards, printed in Rouen. The

A pack of French playing cards

pictures on them were so beautiful that she was sure Master Fetterlock would like to see them. They were quite new. Messer Antonio Bari had brought them as a present only last night.

'Last night!' exclaimed Thomas Fetterlock. 'Did you say "last night"?'

Mistress Bradshaw replied that she had indeed said

'last night'. Messer Antonio had arrived quite unex-
pectedly from Winchester, almost wet through, poor
man. He had supped and slept and gone on his way to
London this forenoon.

Nicholas met his father's eye. By no stretch of imagi-
nation could Newbury be counted on the way between
Winchester and London, and Messer Antonio had said
clearly that he was riding Londonwards.

Supper was a dull meal. This time Cecily was not
allowed to stay up, and her father was moody and silent,
unlike his usual self. The minstrels' gallery was empty
and as Thomas Fetterlock talked to his hostess his voice
echoed thinly in the empty hall. He spoke of the visit to
Burford which, it was planned, Cecily and her parents
were soon to make, and described the joy with which
his wife looked forward to it. If Master Bradshaw could
bring his hawk and his hounds, he could promise some
rare good sport in the forest of Wychwood.

But even to this Master Bradshaw did not respond.
He remarked gruffly that perchance he might excuse
himself. There were pressing matters of business in
Newbury. Nicholas went to bed full of gloomy fore-
bodings. Everything was so different from the last
happy visit.

But the next morning was brighter. The sun shone
and Master Bradshaw had recovered his good humour.
At the very last moment Cecily contrived to waylay
Nicholas and draw him aside into the stable.

'I must speak with you,' she said urgently. 'It is not
true, is it, that your father is in peril of being expelled
from the Staple?'

'Expelled from the Staple?' repeated Nicholas. 'Of
course it is not true. Whatever made you think of such a
thing?'

'Robin heard my father telling my mother.' She peeped round to make sure that they were alone. 'We were playing hide-and-seek, and he was hid in the herb garden. My father caught him and sent him to bed. Oh, Nicholas, are you sure? I have been so truly worried.'

'Of course I am sure. Who can have said such a thing?' But even as he asked the question he was sure of the answer.

'It was Messer Antonio who told my father,' she replied.

'I'll spit him like a chicken,' cried Nicholas with sudden savagery. 'By my Hood of Green, I'll –'

'Hush-sh!' gasped Cecily, shocked. 'Not that oath. That's a terrible oath. I don't know what it means, but my mother says that it is most terrible.'

'I don't care,' growled Nicholas. 'The worse the oath the more I swear it. By my Hood of Green – by Cock and Pie – May Heaven be my witness –'

Cecily caught his arm. 'Don't say that I told you,' she pleaded.

Nicholas shook himself free. 'My father must know. Whatever happens my father must know.'

Just then, from the front of the house, they heard voices calling.

'The horses are there,' cried Nicholas. 'I must go. Don't trouble yourself, my poppet. I shall tell my father, but I'll see that no harm shall come to you.'

Only after he had flung himself into the saddle did it occur to him that he had called Cecily his 'poppet'. That had been his mother's name for him when he was small, and it was the first term of endearment that came to his lips. The odd part was that he had used it to Cecily.

*

He rode beside his father without speaking till they were out of the park and half-way up the hill. Then Master Fetterlock looked at him.

'Well,' he inquired, 'did you enjoy your visit to Beechampton?'

Nicholas shook his head. 'It was different this time.'

'So you noticed it too? Methought that everyone was strangely out of humour. I did not even see the little boy. He was being punished for something.'

'Yes, sir. He had hidden in the herb garden and heard that which he should not have heard.' He plucked up courage. 'There is something, father, which I should tell you.'

'It is not that for which young Robin was punished I trust?'

'I ask your pardon, sir, but this is not just idle prating.'

Master Fetterlock frowned. 'Well, boy, if you must, say on.'

Nicholas took a deep breath and repeated what Cecily had told him. His father looked startled.

'So *that* was it,' he said. 'It seems that Messer Antonio would discredit me for fear lest I might discredit him. Upon my word, I had thought him my friend, but I am afraid that he is in truth my enemy.'

Nicholas was too worried even to want to remark 'it is as I told you!' He plucked up his courage once more.

'Sir,' he pleaded, 'it is not true what they have said?' After he had spoken he held his breath, waiting for the storm to break. But his father spoke gently.

'No, my son, it is not true, though I will not disguise from you that I have sundry troubles with the Staple. These bearded sarplers were not the first. That is why I am at such pains to trace the wool that is going astray.

The good Masters of the Staple are stern with their laws. All the same I shall have an account to settle with Messer Antonio. He has gone to London. Methinks that I had best follow him there, to make him cease his clacking tongue.'

He paused for a moment, and then spoke in a low voice, as though to himself. 'I pray to all the Saints that nothing may hinder that bethrothal.'

Nicholas was startled. 'The betrothal? Sir, has something been said against it? I thought that it was all settled.'

'No, my son, nothing has been said. On the contrary, too little was said this time. It may be that Messer Antonio's words are bearing fruit. The contract was to have been signed on their visit to Burford.'

'But surely they are coming to Burford?' cried Nicholas in alarm. 'Cecily said so, and Mistress Bradshaw said so too.'

'Yes, they are coming to Burford – unless the visit should be cancelled later. But you notice one thing. Master Bradshaw said that he might excuse himself. And without Master Bradshaw, no contract can be signed.'

Mistress Fetterlock began her preparations

Chapter 17

ILL NEWS FROM CALAIS

Two days after their return Master Fetterlock set out for London again, promising that he would be home in time to receive the Bradshaws. Before he left he was closeted first with Giles, then with Leach, and then with Giles again.

Finally he called Nicholas to his counting-house.

'I have seen Leach and questioned him,' he said. 'He was glum and I could get nothing from him. Then, when I charged him with concealing something, he said that he had an aching tooth.'

'An aching tooth has nothing to do with bearded sacks,' said Nicholas scornfully.

'He admitted that he had been careless in the labourers he hired,' said Thomas Fetterlock somewhat wearily. 'Two of them had filled sacks with refuse and, apparently, stolen the good wool. It may be true, but it is scarce enough to account for all the mischief. I did not like his manner. He wriggled like a trapped eel, so that I could not grasp him anywhere.'

'I believe that the good wool is in that barn of his,' asserted Nicholas boldly. 'Can you not force him to show you what he has there?'

Master Fetterlock shook his head. 'It is his own barn. He bought the land and built it. Only the Justices could make him open it against his will. I could dismiss him, but since we want to find the truth that would be more hindrance than help. Giles will watch him like a cat, and I also have a son who is very wide awake. As for me, I must speed to London, to make Messer Antonio curb his tongue. That is a matter more pressing than any.'

With an uneasy mind Nicholas watched his father ride away. It was true that he was now in his father's confidence, sharing his father's secrets, and was no longer treated as a prattling child. But the clouds, instead of lifting, seemed to be closing in, and behind them lurked the threatening shadow of the Lombards, to whom his father was in debt, for whose trade he had been forced to pledge his credit, and who now seemed anxious to break his reputation and sully his good name. He was not even certain that his father's life would be safe if he opposed them. Try as he would the picture kept recurring to his mind of the Lombards on that famous evening when Uncle John arrived, and how readily their hands had flown to their daggers.

The only comfort was that there was no longer such intense secrecy about it. Giles knew most of the story, and before he left, his father told Nicholas that he had discussed it all with Master Richard Chauncellor, the priest. If Nicholas needed help or advice he could go for it to the vicarage.

But if there were troubles afoot, Mistress Fetterlock

was completely oblivious of them. Her whole life was bounded by the prospect of the Bradshaws' visit. She began her preparations as soon as she was informed of it, and if it had been the King and the whole court that was coming, she could not have made more to do. Was not Mistress Bradshaw an heiress, a lady of coat armour, and was not Master Bradshaw, in his wife's right, Lord of the Manor of Beechampton? She spent all her spare time in embroidering a rich cover for the bed in the great chamber to display Mistress Bradshaw's arms – making Nicholas hot with embarrassment and indignation by announcing that one day it would do for him, since he, too, would be able to show his wife's parentage instead of a mere merchant's mark.

The thing that amazed Nicholas about all this was that she was preparing as though the visit were to last for months. And why not? she exclaimed indignantly. A girl bride usually came to live with her future mother-in-law to be taught the ways of the family. Nicholas said no more. Ever since the last visit to Newbury, he felt that his betrothal was pretty uncertain, and like everything else depended upon the solution of his father's problems.

The worst part was that there seemed so little that he could do about it. He and Giles and Hal followed Leach's movements like a pack of bloodhounds, and one day, while Giles took Leach far away on to the wolds towards Stow, the two boys made a determined effort to get into the new barn. But it was built like a fortress, with narrow slits for windows, and the great doors were firmly locked. Hal put his shoulder against them and banged till the rafters echoed, and the cocks and hens fled screeching through a hole in the wall, too small to admit anything but themselves. It was lucky, said Nicholas, that the barn was miles from anywhere, or the noise would have roused all the neighbours.

It was tantalizing to walk round and round the closed building, feeling sure that inside lay the answer to all their questions. On the second time round Hal discovered a tiny door hidden behind an elder bush. But that was as securely fastened as the big one – in fact, said Hal, it was firmer. It had no keyhole, so apparently it must be barred or bolted on the inside.

Trapball

So there was nothing to do but be patient, and for Nicholas the days drifted by, one by one, with the usual things happening, lessons, practice at the butts – for Cecily's skill had put him on his mettle – games of trap ball or stool ball with other boys, or bathing in the river on hot summer afternoons.

It was when he went home one evening with his hair still lanky and dripping that he found two horses tethered in the stable-yard. One was the grey mare usually ridden by Dickon. The second, a strange horse. He had no doubt at all that his father had come home, and he hastily pressed his hair into shape, pulled up his hose and pulled down his doublet before he ventured eagerly through the courtyard and into the hall.

Standing in the window his mother was reading a letter. A manservant waited before her, cap in hand. Nicholas recognized at once the blue livery with three golden stars which was the badge of the Bradshaws of Beechampton. Knowing that in such company his mother would require a show of manners, Nicholas dropped on one knee and remained there until she signalled him to rise and with the same hand dismissed the Bradshaws' man.

As soon as they were alone she sank on to a chair, pushing the letter towards him.

'You may read it,' she said. 'Mistress Bradshaw writes that they will arrive here tomorrow. She is bringing Cecily and her waiting woman, and the blessed Saints alone know how many serving men. The strange part is that his Mastership will not be with them. She pleads that he has business in Salisbury and that he will ride this way later to convey them home again. Would you not expect that such a great man would himself bring his daughter to her betrothal? There is a letter from him for your father. Perchance he may explain in that. I have a mind to open it.'

'But my father? Is he not here?'

'No, nor like to be. He has gone again to Calais, by your leave. Things never happen singly. Almost at the same time as the messenger from Beechampton, Dickon arrived home. Methinks your father's senses must have left him. He knew that the maid and her parents would come to Burford, and yet he excuses himself. For this marriage making, it seems, we have only women, and not a father on either side. I know not what to make of it.'

Nicholas worked his way through the scrolls and flourishes of Mistress Bradshaw's letter with difficulty. It told him nothing fresh and, deep in thought, he laid it back on the table.

'As if that were not enough,' she continued, 'with Dickon your father has sent your Uncle John, recommending me that I should give him lodging, as he has been sick of the smallpox.'

'Uncle John? He is here?'

'He has gone to the hospital,' she replied calmly. 'When he learned of the cause that we are in, and of the company we shall have tomorrow, he said that he would go to the Brothers. He would have good rest there for a few days before he rides on to Bristol.' Noting the look of disapproval on her son's face, she began to excuse herself. 'God knows he is my brother, and most welcome and loving to me always. But he could not have come at a worse time. What can I do when the house will be full, and he but recently with the smallpox too? The hospital is a house for sick travellers. The good Brethren will make him welcome, and serve him better than he could be served here. You may go and see him. The contagion is past, so he did tell me.'

Nicholas was shocked. In spite of her excuses he knew that Uncle John was an unwelcome guest because the Bradshaws were coming, just as he had been when the Lombards came. Taking her permission as given, he turned and made for the door. His mother called him back, warning him not to forget that the hospice was closed by now. The gates were shut after Vespers, except to travellers. Then, seeing that he was determined to go, she held out to him another letter, its seals still unbroken. Even across the room he recognized his father's neat handwriting.

'If you are going,' she said, 'will you speed this to Master Richard at the vicarage. Dickon has ridden without rest, and he is weary.'

Nicholas's heart leaped. He did not need to be told twice. Here would be news at last. He seized the letter and with the hastiest of bows hurried out into the road, reading the superscription as he went:

To the right worshipful and reverend Master Richard Chauncellor in Burford, be this delivered in haste.

*

As soon as he was out of sight of the windows he took to his heels, pounding down the hill with great strides. A bare glance sufficed to show him that the gates of the hospital were in truth closed, though he would not in any case have stopped, not even for Uncle John. As he passed he heard the wail of Hal's bagpipe in the shop of his uncle, Nash, the barber chirugeon. Apparently he had been called to drown some poor patient's yells.

Master Richard was pacing the garden, saying his office. He gave Nicholas his book to hold while he broke the seals. Watching his face Nicholas saw his brow crease in a frown, and he could scarcely curb his impatience while the priest read the letter through a second time.

He looked up at Nicholas, lips grimly compressed.

'I fear that it is trouble, my son,' he said. 'Your good

father has been called to Calais to answer further charges. This letter was written before he started, but since his summons came from the Mayor of the Staple himself, he fears that things may go ill with him.'

'What is it?' asked Nicholas quickly. 'Is it once more the bearded sarplers?'

Master Richard shook his head. 'This time it is a different matter. You know that your father stood as surety for Messer Bari and his company, that they might send certain wool to Italy over land? The terms of the pledge state that it shall not be offered for sale north of the mountains.'

Nicholas nodded. Yes, his father had told him that.

'Well, it seems that an officer of the Staple, who chanced to visit the city of Rouen, in Normandy, found in the mart some sarplers bearing the Fetterlock mark. These had not passed through Calais, and your father has no ships of his own. Therefore there is no doubt that they are part of the consignment to the Lombards for which your father offered the pledge. He may himself escape censure, though as he is already in trouble with the Staple, he fears that they will not spare him. But in any case it will cost him a great sum of money, for they will claim his surety; and a great sum of money is not easy to find.'

Nicholas stood frowning. 'Do you mean, sir, that Messer Bari has done this deliberately – actually broken his trust knowing that if it were found my father would bear the hurt of it?'

'I fear that is the truth,' said Master Richard gravely.

'Then before God he is a traitor and a false knave,' cried Nicholas.

'Curb your tongue, my son,' warned the priest. 'Hard words help not at all. I still cannot see what the

Lombard gains by breaking this trust. Tell me, Nicholas, did you not see this wool at Southampton? Were there none other than the sarplers that were pledged?'

'The galley had already sailed. But my father saw the lists at the Wool House. He said that they were counted aright.'

'Ah! well, I am not satisfied that we have got to the bottom of it. Remember it in your prayers, my son. I will offer a Mass for your father, and do you pray for my intention.'

There was little sleep for Nicholas that night. He lay tossing till daylight came, then fell asleep, and woke with a start to find the sun shining bright. Leaping from his bed, he leaned out of the window to judge the hour. To his left and farther down the hill stood the Hospice of St John the Evangelist where Augustinian friars nursed the sick and housed poor travellers. Uncle John was there and he had not yet seen him. On the still morning air the sound of voices chanting came to him from their little chapel. They must be saying the office of Prime. That meant six o'clock. He remembered that the gate, shut at Vespers, was opened again after Prime, so he slipped into shirt and hose, pulled on an old warm jerkin instead of his doublet, and, shoes in hand, tiptoed downstairs.

But though the hospice gates were open, the brother whom he met, with two yoked buckets, fetching water, told him that he could not see any of the inmates until after the first Mass, which was in half an hour. Remembering Master Richard's exhortation, Nicholas spent the time on his knees, begging the help of every saint with an altar or a light in the chapel. His uncle, with a grin of pleased astonishment, found him there. After the Mass they retired to the cloister, and sat on a low

*One of the Brothers
fetching water*

wall overlooking the sunny garth where white doves strutted on the grass.

The sight of Uncle John's pitted face gave Nicholas a shock. In truth he had suffered from the smallpox. But John Stern made light of it. Any man who lived for long in the city must be prepared for that, he declared. He was lucky that it was not the pestilence.

There was only one subject about which he wanted to talk – the voyage of Cristoforo Colombo. He spoke of it with pride in what had been achieved by an old shipmate, and also with fury that the English King had let the credit for it slip through his fingers. He had seen the King, and even now there was a hope that money might be granted to him and to Master Cabot to sail to the north-west, and discover, not islands as Colombo had done, but the mainland of the Continent of Asia. He would rest at the hospice a day or two. Then he would be away again, to Bristol, to get the plans afoot.

He remembered, at the end, to tease Nicholas about the coming of his bride-to-be. He must see the maid, he declared. All sailors had an eye for a comely wench.

Nicholas reached home at the same moment as his mother, who had been to Mass at the parish church, and who, thinking that he was newly out of bed, chided him for neglecting his duties. When she heard, with some astonishment, that he had heard Mass at the hospice, she expressed the hope that her brother had slept well. She would go and see him later, but she trusted that he would be wise and rest all day, by which Nicholas understood that she hoped he would not be there when the Bradshaws arrived.

All day long, as fussy as a hen, Mistress Fetterlock thrust upon Nicholas a thousand small tasks. The thyme was in flower by the river; would he please go and pick some, that it might be strewn among the rushes in the bed-chamber. His hair was badly trimmed; he looked a fool without a fringe; would he kindly go to the barber at once. There was not a knife in the house that would carve. Would he take them all down to Wat the cutler to be sharpened; and he must stand by the grindstone till they were done, or they would have never a knife till Christmas.

He endured it all as best he could till, late in the afternoon, he had an inspiration. On the day that they visited Newbury Master Bradshaw had come forth to meet them. Ought not he, as his father was away, to ride out and escort their guests?

Mistress Fetterlock at once agreed. Let him take Dickon, and Hal too, if he wished, to make it more of a ceremony.

Cecily's mother travelled in a litter

Chapter 18

THE MAP

INSTEAD of riding down into the valley, Nicholas halted at the crest of the hill. The wolds stretched on three sides as far as the eye could see, with Leach's barn, a lonely speck, a couple of miles away. In front of them wound the road along which the visitors would come.

They had not waited long when Hal, whose ears were attuned to distant sounds, cried 'Listen'. A few moments later Nicholas too heard the jingle of harness and caught the first glimpse of the travellers as they emerged from behind a clump of trees.

There seemed to be eight or nine horses in the party, though it was hard to pick out one from another. Then as he watched, a white pony detached itself, and came trotting ahead towards him. He touched Petronel with his heels, and started off down the hill. Cecily waved her kerchief and he made Petronel dance on her hind legs in greeting, realizing that once more Cecily had taken all the stiffness out of the business, and that he was at his ease.

Mistress Bradshaw travelled in a litter carried by two horses, and Mistress Lovejoy rode pillion behind a groom. There were four armed guards and two baggage horses. Such a cavalcade travelled slowly and they had spent a night at Faringdon.

Nicholas dismounted to offer his obedience to Cecily's mother who was painfully shocked at her daughter's unseemly behaviour. He offered apologies for his father's absence, but Mistress Bradshaw was so conscious of her own husband's shortcomings that she was almost relieved to hear that her host was missing too. In the end, when the formality of the reception was all over, and Mistress Fetterlock did not abate one jot of its full ceremony, the party of women settled down very happily together, exchanging views on head-dresses, on the shocking vanity of shaving the forehead in order to look wiser than God intended, on stitches for tapestry, and on the all-important question of preserves. Nicholas and Cecily found themselves with the task of picking endless raspberries and currants and gooseberries for their elders to try one another's recipes.

Picking fruit grew dull when they were tired of eating it. Then they discovered that if they picked really hard for an hour they could fill enough baskets to account for the whole morning, and have plenty of time to run down to the river, or across to Meg's cot, or even to saddle Petronel and Meadowsweet. Uncle John appeared one day to pay a ceremonial call on Cecily and her mother, but Mistress Fetterlock was vigilant and the visit did not last long, and then once more the family scattered to bower or orchard.

It was in the orchard that Cecily brought to Nicholas one morning a small parchment roll. She declared that she had brought it from home hidden in the folds of her embroidery, and had quite forgotten it. Robin had sent it to him.

Nicholas spread it out. 'It's a map,' he said, rather obviously.

She nodded, 'I know. It's the map of an island. It almost shames me to tell you, but Robin stole it. He took it from the Lombards.'

'From the Lombards,' Nicholas exclaimed sharply. He looked at the map again. 'What island is it? There are not any names.'

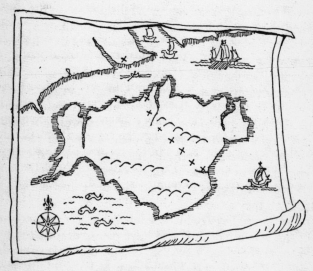

The Map had no names on it

Cecily shook her head. 'We did not know what island it is. Robin thought that it might be the island of Brazil. Do you remember that you said that your uncle was going there, and that he was afraid that the Lombards might get there first? Well, Robin found this map.

Messer Antonio dropped it the last time he came; that was the night before you stayed on your way back from Southampton. Robin wanted to give it to you then, but he did not see you. He thought your Uncle John might like to look at it.'

Nicholas stared at the map, but he could make nothing of it.

'Shall we take it to Uncle John?' he proposed. 'He is still at the hospital. I know a back way into the garden; no one need see us.'

To slip across the road and over some stepping-stones in the wall, into the woods at the back of the hospice was easy enough. By good fortune they encountered Uncle John himself cutting up a felled tree as an offering of gratitude to the good brothers who had given him hospitality. He stuck his axe into the wood when he saw them and invited them to sit down on the trunk.

Urged by Nicholas, Cecily repeated her story about the map, a little shamefaced as she confessed that Robin had stolen it. John Stern in the meanwhile was studying the parchment. As she mentioned the Island of Brazil a smile played round the corners of his mouth. But he waited until she had finished.

'That is a pretty story, Mistress,' he commented. 'I take it very kindly that you and your brother should interest yourselves in my poor fortunes. But, alack! the map is not of the Island of Brazil, or any other distant isle. It is much nearer than that. It shows none other than the Isle of Wight.'

'The Isle of Wight,' cried Nicholas, pressing closer. 'Why, that is nigh to Southampton. Is Southampton marked on the map?'

'Nothing is marked,' said Uncle John, his brow puckered. 'There are no names. There is no mark for

Southampton, nor any for Newport, which are the two great harbours. It is all passing strange. There is a small cross here, which I take it is a little place called Leap, whence some people go to the island. It is an ancient quay. Some say the Romans built it. There is another mark at the end of the sea passage at Gurnard's Bay on the island, though again there is no name. Then there are several marks across the isle and one more cross by the village of Shanklin on the far side. I can make nothing of it. It seems to be an ordinary map; not very well drawn, perchance, but quite clear.'

'Are you sure that it is the Isle of Wight?' persisted Nicholas.

'A plague on you, boy, of course I'm sure,' returned his uncle irritably. 'Have I not sailed every creek of these waters. Here is the East Cow and the West Cow as you sail up to Newport, and this great inlet, just by Leap, is the river leading up to Beaulieu. . . .'

'Beaulieu?' broke in Cecily suddenly. 'The Abbey of Beaulieu?'

He showed her the map. 'The Abbey is not marked, Mistress, but it would be here – at the head of the creek. When I was a boy –' He launched upon a story which on another day would have delighted Nicholas. But at that moment they heard unmistakably the distant sound of a voice calling. It was the voice of Mistress Fetterlock.

Quickly Nicholas grabbed the map from his uncle, and bundled Cecily ahead of him, across the wall and by a side track into the stable-yard, from which they emerged to receive a scolding for making themselves smelly with the horses instead of filling their baskets with raspberries.

Later, when dinner was finished, they returned to the

orchard to talk it all over. Both of them were full of suppressed excitement.

'Did you notice,' said Cecily eagerly, 'that he said Beaulieu?'

Nicholas nodded. 'I did notice,' he said. 'It was at Beaulieu that you stayed with your grandparents.'

'Yes, and where I saw your man Leach and Toad-face, with the packhorses. They were not going to Southampton I am certain of that. Do you think that they could have been on their way to that place Leap? Your uncle said there was a quay there.'

'It is possible. The galley might draw in there after it leaves Southampton.'

'But then,' she cried, 'why the map of the Isle of Wight?'

Nicholas suddenly clapped his hands. 'I have it. Of a truth, it is as clear as day. The wool crosses the water from Leap to that bay my uncle spoke of. Then they must carry it over the Island, where there are marks on the map. And the galley waits for them at the other side. Messer Antonio said so; don't you remember?' She looked bewildered so he checked himself and said that he was sorry. He forgot that she had not been there. 'The galley lies off the Isle of Wight to pick up water. It is the ordinary thing. My uncle told us so too. The drinking water there keeps fresh longer than any other. If they should take on board wool as well as water, who is to know?'

'Then that is why the extra wool was not written down at Southampton?'

'Of course. It does not go near Southampton. It pays no taxes, I'll be bound. Messer Antonio's thirty bales are all honest and aboveboard. He can answer any questions about those, and he can do what he likes with the rest, because nobody knows that it exists. Oh if only I could find my father.'

'Will he be coming home soon?'

'I know not. He went first to London to seek Messer Antonio, and then the Staple called him to Calais. I can see it all now. When we were at Winchester we were getting very close, and Messer Antonio must have feared that my father suspected him. Therefore he tried to harm my father before my father could harm him. That was why he said false things of him. If men should think that my father is a knave they will not heed what he should say of others.'

Cecily nodded again. 'It is true,' she said. 'But how about the wool? How does that get there? When I saw those packhorses in the Forest, where had they come from?'

'From Leach,' cried Nicholas, suddenly inspired. 'Child, however it is done, by fair means or foul, we must see the inside of Leach's barn.'

*

The obvious thing was to do as his father had said and take the matter to Master Richard. So Nicholas set off forthwith for the parsonage, taking the map with him. Once more the priest was in the garden. He listened carefully and with mounting excitement to Nicholas's story. Half-way through he drew him indoors and spread the map on his desk. It was all quite clear, he declared at the end of the recital. There did not seem to be the shadow of a doubt. This map was the key to the whole matter. He would write a letter to Master Fetterlock and send it by a swift messenger.

'But the barn, sir. We must see inside the barn. Could we not beg the justices to break down the doors?'

The priest shook his head. 'Not so fast, my son. We have no proof. The chain is not yet forged in all its links. You must have patience.'

Nicholas sighed – a sigh of exasperation. How could he have patience when the very proof that they sought was without doubt inside the barn? Master Richard looked at his rebellious face.

'I told you to pray, my son,' he said. 'And look what has come of your prayer. This map has, like a miracle, been put into your hands. Now, do you go into the church, and into the chapel of the holy St Thomas of Canterbury, your father's patron. Ask that he will obtain this favour for you.'

Nicholas entered the church. He went seldom to the chapel of St Thomas, even for his father's sake, because it was raised several steps above a vault, where, so his nurse had told him, they had buried all the skeletons of

Nicholas found the ladies gathered in the garden

people who died centuries ago. Today, he took hold on himself, climbed the steps and kneeled alone in the little chapel behind the carved screens. Tiny lamps twinkled before the altar, and glinted on ornaments

of gold and silver, thankofferings from the people of
Burford who had made the pilgrimage to Canterbury
and come safely home, their prayers answered. A
painting on the wall showed the murder of the Saint by
the four knights with drawn swords. He found himself
thinking that no one could possibly swing a sword like
that; then he steadied himself, whispered his petition,
and hurried back into the open air. Cecily would be
impatient to hear how he had got on.

To his dismay he found all the ladies gathered in the
garden with lute and viol and sweetmeats and a story
book to read aloud, and for hours there was no chance
to speak to Cecily alone. At last however, as the sun began to sink, the gnats and little biting flies became his
friends. In the general business of carrying indoors
cushions and stools and musical instruments he was
able to whisper a word to Cecily, and arrange to meet
her afterwards in the orchard.

He had hardly begun to tell her what the priest had
said when footsteps came blundering through the gate
that led into the orchard from the stable-yard. It was
Hal.

Nicholas looked at him in astonishment, for in
Cecily's presence Hal as a rule was a shy and speechless
servant. Yet here he was breaking into the garden,
where he never came without leave, so red and breath-
less and excited, that for a moment Nicholas wondered
if he had drunk too much ale.

'Young master, look!' he cried. 'See what I have got.
Mistress, see!' He spread his big hand before them.
Across the palm lay a large iron key.

Nicholas's mouth fell open with astonishment. An
idea shot into his head, but he said nothing aloud. It
could not, it simply could not be.

It was Cecily who asked, 'What is it?'

'It is the key of Leach's barn,' said Hal, and waited to watch the effect of his words.

Whether it was really a miracle or not, they had to listen how it had taken place. Leach had come that afternoon to the barber's shop with his aching tooth. Hal's uncle had said that there was no help for it; the tooth must come out. Leach was a big man, so he had

Leach loses a tooth

sent for helpers to hold him down. The tooth was stubborn and the struggle long drawn out. While it was going on, Hal had looked down and seen the key, slipped from the packer's loosened belt, lying on the floor. He had put his foot on it quickly, and, dazed with the pain, the wretched man had gone off without noticing his loss.

Nicholas found his voice. 'Come on,' he cried. 'We must go at once. Come on, to the barn.'

But it wasn't as easy as all that. Leach had discovered the loss as soon as he got home, and sent a messenger back to the barber's. It was only by quips and japes and something very like lies that Hal had succeeded in holding on to the key. His uncle had seen that he had it, and the best he could manage was to send back a message that he, Hal, would bring the key to Leach's house at Westwell within the hour. It was madness for them all to go to the barn. Leach might be on the look-out. If Hal went alone he could try to slip into the barn on the way and see what was inside.

Nicholas was distracted, but whatever way they looked at it, Hal was right. They must let him go without them, and there was no time to lose.

The hardest thing of all was to go indoors, eat supper calmly, and settle to a game of backgammon. Nicholas kept getting up and going to the window till his mother asked him what ailed him. When he said that he was hot and must go outside for some air, she bade him sternly stay where he was. He must have an ague. She would give him a rhubarb potion when he went to bed. He caught Cecily's eye, twinkling merrily, but for once it irritated him. It was all very well for her to look upon it as a joke. It was not her father who was in trouble.

At last he stood alone by the window of his bedchamber at the top of the house. With some skill he had tipped the rhubarb potion into an open chest of dried herbs in his mother's still-room, where she had mixed the brew. She might find them wet in the morning, but rhubarb had no smell, and anyhow he did not care. Softly he unlatched the casement and stood looking down into the road.

Presently he was rewarded. It was by the light of a half-moon that he saw a figure move and a pale face turned upwards. He waved a kerchief as a signal and crept downstairs.

Hal was waiting by the yard door.

'I got into the barn,' he whispered, 'but it was nearly dark. There were sacks – sarplers of wool, all packed and sewn. There were lots of them; it was too dark to count how many.'

'How about the key?' inquired Nicholas anxiously.

'I took it back,' said Hal. 'I could not help it. But it is all right. You remember the little door? I found it and drew back the bar. It is well hidden behind sacks and will not be noticed. We can get in that way at any time.'

The Bridge at Burford

Chapter 19

FEATHERS

NICHOLAS lay awake thinking. At first it seemed to him that they had found all that they needed to know. If Leach's barn were full of stolen wool, he could be taken before the justices, and that would settle everything.

But would it? How could it help his father, who was in trouble about wool found in France, if a dishonest packer was pilloried or beaten or even hanged in Burford? How would it prove that Leach, let alone the Lombards, was guilty of the crimes for which the Staple blamed his father? No. He must find some way of showing that the wool which Leach stole was the same wool which travelled across the Isle of Wight, and turned up in the mart of Rouen. He sat up in bed gazing into the darkness.

Suddenly the solution came to him. The sarplers must be marked. He and Hal must get into Leach's barn and mark them with some secret sign which would pass unnoticed until it was wanted. Then he could tell his father to say to the Staple, 'If the next bales which you find in Rouen mart are marked with such and such a sign, I can tell you exactly how they came there.' He went to sleep at last, feeling almost triumphant.

It was not until he tried to explain his plan to Cecily and Hal that the practical difficulty became obvious. How, inquired Hal, could the sacks be marked so that Leach himself would not notice the marks?

This question worried all three of them and nobody seemed to have an answer. However, Hal had important news. Leach's face was swollen like a pumpkin, and he was riding to Oxford to consult a barber-chirugeon of greater repute than Will Nash. He would be away all day. It was an answer to their prayers. They would be able to get into the barn without fear of interruption.

Cecily begged and begged that they would take her with them. Nicholas objected because it was certain that if her mother knew, Mistress Lovejoy would be sent with her. If she slipped off without permission, as she had done before, she would certainly be missed, for this time they could not hurry. It might take them hours. But Cecily said she did not care. She would far rather have a beating when she came back, than stay at home and miss everything.

So in the end Nicholas said that she could come. Once more the horses were saddled secretly. Hal, mounted on Dickon's mare, went ahead to ride round by Westwell and make sure that Leach had actually started for Oxford. Nicholas and Cecily moved more slowly, keeping as much as possible under the shelter of woods and hills. Nicholas carried in his pouch a metal die of the Fetterlock mark and a pad of ink which he had taken from his father's counting-house. He did not quite know how he could use them, but he hoped that inspiration might come.

In spite of his longer journey, Hal reach the barn ahead of them. As they came over the brow of the hill, he signalled to them that the coast was clear. His horse was hidden among the same clump of thorn trees which had sheltered Nicholas on his last visit; and here they tethered Petronel and Meadowsweet too.

Hal had already tried the little door behind the elder bush. It was still unbarred and there was plenty of room to squeeze in. With a beating heart Nicholas led the way.

It seemed so dark inside that at first he feared they would be able to see nothing. The barn was high like a church and lit only by the shafts of golden sunshine that pierced the slits in the wall. Along these streamers of light motes and cobwebs danced, but behind them the shadows seemed blacker than ever. Hal fumbled his way forward until he stood in the darkest part.

'It's easier here,' he said, his voice echoing among the rafters and startling a roosting hen into an agitated cackle. 'If you shut your eyes for a minute you'll see better afterwards.'

It was true. As they became accustomed to it, the darkness thinned and lightened until they could make out plainly the outlines of a collection of bales, neatly packed and squared, standing in orderly rows at the far end of the barn.

'Here they are,' cried Hal. 'Two, four, six –' he went on, counting aloud – 'twenty. And finest clip, I dare swear. Look, master, they are marked already. There is FL all over them. It looks as though the canvas were stamped before they were made up.'

Nicholas examined them, his eyes now used to the light.

'If I marked them at the bottom,' he said doubtfully, 'it would not be noticed there – and I can use the die crossways to make it different.'

Hal shook his head. 'They are not corded yet,' he said. 'They will turn them about to cord them. For certain they will notice a new mark.'

For some time they argued. Hal wanted to clip a nick in the corner of each sack, and Nicholas still stuck to the idea of his die. In the meanwhile Cecily had been wandering round the barn. She came back to them now, holding something between her closed hands.

'How would these do?' she asked.

Nicholas peered at her. 'What have you got?'

'Feathers,' she answered simply. 'Hen's feathers. There's a sack of them over there. I suppose they are saved for pillows. Could we push a few into each bale? They would stick to the wool.'

'Of a certainty they would,' cried Hal. 'Mistress, you have it. If you once get the feathers among the wool, they will never get them out again.'

Their fortunes seemed to have turned completely. From now everything went right. True that each sarpler had to be opened and sewn up again, but there were clipping shears hanging on one nail, and on another a hank of Arras thread with a packer's needle actually dangling from it. Hal knew the stitch. He had helped with the packing after the clip. And Cecily's hand was small enough to be pushed through a tiny hole. The entire business was finished in an hour or so, and everything tidied away. The sarplers stood in their same rows ready for their journey to France, looking so innocent on their outsides, but each one charged with a good handful of hen's feathers.

They rode home in great spirits. But trouble awaited them. Mistress Bradshaw had hunted for her daughter everywhere, and was convinced that she was either kidnapped or drowned. At the sight of Cecily, alive and very dirty, her mother's sorrow changed to wrath. She demanded to know instantly where the wench had been. Cecily, suddenly inspired, confessed that she had been to see some wool packed. This made matters worse.

'You have ridden abroad, mistress, like any slut, without your mother or your gentlewoman?' raged her angry parent.

It was more than Nicholas could stand. He stepped forward.

'Madame, I ask your pardon,' he said, suddenly bold. 'If so be that Mistress Cecily shall be the wife of a Wool Stapler, it is fitting that she should know the business of it. *I* took her this morning to the packing. I beg of you, if you are angered, to remember that the fault is mine.'

Cecily's mother and his own both gazed at him in astonished silence. Then Mistress Bradshaw told her daughter to go to her bed. When Cecily had gone, Nicholas also bowed deeply and withdrew.

As he closed the door he heard his mother's voice in the room behind him.

'They say that men children take after their mothers, but I tell you, madam, today you have seen my husband.'

*

Sitting about and waiting, after so much excitement, was very hard to bear, particularly as Nicholas had decided that no one must be told the secret of the barn. He longed to blurt it out to Giles, or Master Richard, or to Uncle John, who left for Bristol the next day. But it would not be safe. If anybody knew that Leach's barn was full of stolen wool, they might feel bound to inform the justices. Everyone had a duty to stop or arrest a thief, and a whole village could be fined for neglecting that duty.

Then Leach would be taken, and the whole plan would fall through.

Hal promised to keep a watch on the barn, and on Leach too. He could go in and out at any hour without being asked awkward questions, and there were always the sheep to give him an excuse for wandering across the wolds. He came every evening to report to Nicholas, but it was always the same story. The sacks were still there. Nothing had changed.

But at last one night, when Nicholas had just got into his bed, he heard a long soft note on a shepherd's pipe beneath his window. The moon had risen and the street outside was brilliantly lit. One glance was enough to show him Hal standing in the shadow below. Nicholas flung on his clothes and tiptoed downstairs. There was a light showing under the door of his mother's bower and he held his breath as he passed, praying that she had not heard Hal's whistle. If Bel should bark now all would be lost. But all was well. Behind the closed door there was silence.

Hal was panting with excitement. 'They are going tonight,' he stammered. 'I've been over to Westwell to have a look round, and I saw Toad-face at Leach's house. They have about a dozen packhorses and the moon is full. I'll swear they'll be gone before dawn. Come quickly, and we'll get to the trees and watch them.'

Nicholas needed no second bidding. They set off at once, running across the wolds, for they dared not ride.

On foot it seemed a long way and they had to slow down their pace because of the uneven ground. As they approached the crest of the hill Hal signed to Nicholas to drop low, lest they should be visible against the sky. They crept the last hundred yards on all fours, and lay down thankfully among the inky shadows of the thorn trees.

In front of them the barn, silvery white, was bathed in moonlight, almost as clear as day. It was quite deserted. For a few minutes they remained completely silent, but there was no sound except the rustle of tiny creatures of the night and, far away in the valley, the long hoot of an owl.

'Perhaps they will not come until the morrow,' whispered Nicholas.

At that instant Hal's warning hand gripped his arm. Something was moving on the hill-side beyond the barn. They strained their eyes to pierce the even pallor of the moonlight. Then they heard a tiny jingle, and another, and another. A man's voice called 'Steady, there', and one by one a line of packhorses came into view, silhouetted against the light wall of the barn. Then two men rode up and halted; one was on a dark horse, a shadowy figure, hardly visible, though they guessed that it was Toad-face; the second showed up clearly, a sharp pattern of black and white. It was Leach on his piebald mare.

From the cover of the thorn trees they watched spellbound as he dismounted and unlocked the great main doors. They could hear the creak as he opened them wide. He called out something, they could not catch what, and two or three men appeared on foot from among the horses and vanished inside the barn. Somebody kindled a light, and soon a couple of lanterns

From the cover of thorn trees

shone in the dark interior, moving about like glow-worms. Then the horses were led up to the door, one at a time, and the sarplers carried out and strapped on. Leach issued orders in his normal voice; the drovers answered, spoke to their horses, laughed or swore as though, in that remote spot, there was no need for caution.

Once Leach came out of the barn and stood gazing round him, as though he were searching the skyline. He seemed to fix upon the thorn trees and for what seemed an endless moment he stared at them. Nicholas heard Hal catch his breath. Could he have spotted them? It almost appeared as if he must have done.

Then he turned away again. They heard him call out, 'just after midnight I should hazard,' and they realized that he was reckoning the time by the moon.

At last all the bales were loaded – they counted twenty of them. In the stillness of the night they heard the key grate in the lock of the door. The drovers marshalled the procession, and slowly, in single file, it moved away towards the south. The feathers had started for France.

Nicholas and Hal stirred painfully. They were stiff and cold. Though the scene that they had watched was the climax of all their plans, they were too tired even to feel excited, and they plodded home almost in silence.

Back in his bed Nicholas lay and waited for the dawn. There was one more thing that he had to do. When daylight came he must write to his father.

*

The letter went away under seal with one from Master Richard. The priest heard the story with amazement, saying nothing except an occasional 'Good! Good!' At the end his counsel was simple. He told them to be patient, and to pray.

But to be patient yet once again was very hard. There had been so much waiting. At first they talked of nothing else whenever they were together, Nicholas and Hal, or Nicholas and Cecily, or all three of them. They were certain that something exciting would happen soon; there must surely be news from somewhere. But day passed after day without anything out of the ordinary taking place. Leach reappeared and no one mentioned that he had ever been away. Of Master Fetterlock there was no word at all. It seemed that he was still delayed in Calais.

Then suddenly there came a letter which nobody had expected. Master Bradshaw wrote to ask pardon that he was unable to come to Burford and to suggest that it was time that his wife and daughter returned home. Cecily was in despair. To go home now, and never to see what happened next was just more than she could bear. She and Nicholas put their heads together. Master Richard was brought into it, and in the end Mistress Fetterlock suggested to Mistress Bradshaw that Cecily might remain behind to learn the housewifely arts, since a maid learned more easily from one who was not her own mother. Mistress Bradshaw was a little doubtful, but Cecily coaxed and pleaded and promised that she would work faithfully, and at last her mother agreed to let her stay.

But if Nicholas and Cecily had imagined that they would have time to themselves, they were mistaken. Mistress Fetterlock was in her element, and Cecily found herself occupied from morning till night. She cooked, she sewed, she spun, she wove linen to put in her own dower chest, or wound bobbins for Mistress Fetterlock's loom; and in the intervals she went to church.

Nicholas, feeling himself left out, returned to the sheep. Although winter was still a long way off, already the flocks were being sorted, the breeding ewes given the best pasture, the yearlings for next season's clip driven on to the uplands to thicken their fleeces, and those whose skins were doomed to provide wool-fells marked for the Martinmas killing. The walls of the sheep-folds were repaired, the barns cleaned out and made water-tight. Over the stone roofs of the little town the autumn mists lingered, and the smoke of evening fires mounted in their blue columns.

Cecily found herself occupied from morning to night

It was on such an autumn evening that Master Fetter-lock returned.

Nicholas heard of it first as he hung over the parapet of the stone bridge dangling a line into the water. The baker's journeyman came by, perched grotesquely on top of two sacks of meal from the miller, all draped over an old white horse. Nicholas moved into one of the angles of the bridge to allow them room to pass. But with a 'Whoa there!' the man stopped and called out to him.

'Young master, do you know that your father has come home?'

For a moment Nicholas scarcely took it in. Then, calling his thanks over his shoulder, he started to run up the long hill. He did not stop to think that he was dirty and unbrushed, but plunged through the entry and into the hall. In his excitement all remembrance of the courtesies left him. He bounded across the room and stood panting before his father.

Thomas Fetterlock put his hands on Nicholas's shoulders.

'My son,' he said, with his steady smile. 'Of a truth you have served me well.'

*

It was not until supper was over and the board cleared that Master Fetterlock attempted to tell them what had happened. Then, in his tall chair, before a blazing faggot, a mug of mulled ale in his hand, he began his story. Mistress Fetterlock, on a cushioned seat, twirled her spindle. Cecily, on a low stool, fed the fire with stalks of spent lavender. Nicholas, frankly idle, hugged his knees and gazed spellbound at his father.

'When I left Burford,' Master Fetterlock began, 'I rode full speed to London, determined to find Messer Antonio and demand from him the reason why he had said ill things about me with intent to destroy my fame and fortune. I went straight to the lodging where the Lombards are wont to lie. But there I learned that Messer Bari, who had been there for a week, had left that very morning for Southampton. Since I was now suspicious of the Lombards I wondered why he should go there so soon again, until I remembered that another galley was due from Flanders, on its way home to Italy. You recall, my son, that they told us about it at the port?'

Nicholas nodded without speaking, his eyes never moving from his father's face.

'It seemed natural enough then that Messer Antonio should go to meet it. But in London wherever I went I met the same story about myself, spread by the Lombards, that Master Fetterlock of the Staple was on the rocks and heading for disaster. It was having its effect. Here and there I found old customers who were loath to trade with me. Then I received another summons from Calais, to answer the same old charge of bearded sarplers – more and more of them, full of every sort of refuse. I saw the Mayor of the Staple, and pleaded a dishonest packer. He accepted my plea, but I had to pledge everything I possessed, and more, to pay for the wrong. But I cleared it all up and was awaiting ship to come home when fresh trouble started. I believe you have heard of it, my son?'

'Is it that which you wrote to Master Richard about, the mart at Rouen?' asked Nicholas.

His father nodded. 'That is it,' he said. 'By chance – I had almost said "by mischance", though now it is a good thing that it all happened; I say again, by chance, a Staple officer happened to go to the mart at Rouen. He found there sacks of perfect Cots wool, carrying the Fetterlock mark. When he returned to Calais he put the matter before the Council of the Staple. It was declared certain that this was part of that pack of wool which the Lombards were licensed to carry over the mountains to Italy, and for which I had offered myself as surety. Not only must I pay up the surety of five hundred pounds, but the Council believed that I was in the plot with the Lombards. They pointed out that the wool which I sent to Calais and Bruges, though labelled and charged as finest Cotswold was false trash. But the wool in Rouen was beautiful stuff – the pick of the clip. It was natural that they should believe that it was my own doing. They put me into the prison of the keep at Calais, to await my trial. There I lay I know not how long. It must have been for weeks. I thought that I was finished, until they brought me a letter from my son.'

He paused to smile at Nicholas.

'That letter entirely changed my fortunes. It told, so clearly that even my Masters of the Staple had no doubt, how the good wool had travelled from the dishonest packer's barn, across the Isle of Wight, escaping customs, and thence by Lombard galley to the marts of France. But above all it offered proof that when the next sacks should follow by the same route they would be marked. The Mayor sent a messenger to Rouen, and sure enough the wool appeared, all decorated with chickens' feathers. That was a wonderful touch – true woman's wit. It strikes me, Mistress Cecily, that if I have a son of which I am proud, I may some day have a daughter who is a match for him.'

Cecily's eyes sparkled; her whole face was bright with gladness. There was a moment's pause. Then Mistress Fetterlock said, a trifle sharply, that she had known none of this. It was strange that the children had not told her. And what was the next to happen? Was the matter now finished?

'The next is,' said her husband, 'that I ride to London once again and that Nicholas comes with me.'

At this there was a general stir. Mistress Fetterlock again asked questions. What would they do in London? And what had happened to the Lombards?

'The Lombards are in charge of the Mayor of the Staple. They lie, I believe, in the prison of the Marshalsea in London. There is to be a trial before the Council in the Guildhall of the City of London. I am sent to convey the chief witness.'

Nicholas looked at him in doubt. Even now he was not quite clear about it all.

'Who is the chief witness?' he asked. 'Is he Master Leach?'

His father shook his head. 'Master Leach will ride with us,' he said. 'But with this difference, that he will ride in custody, to join the Lombards as prisoners at the bar. The chief witness, my son, is a man of honour. His name is Nicholas Fetterlock.'

POSTSCRIPT

BEFORE you put this book down you might like to know a little more about the pictures, and some of the places mentioned in the story.

Burford still stands on the hill sloping down to the river Windrush just as it did in Nicholas's day. It is of course bigger than it was then, but you can see in Sheep Street the house which I have drawn as 'Fetterlock House'. There are other houses opposite it now, but from Nicholas's bedroom window you would doubtless still be able to look over the roofs to the trees of the Hospice of St John the Evangelist, as it then was, when Uncle John was cared for by the Augustinian brothers. Master Richard Chauncellor really was Vicar of Burford in 1493, and in the church you can see the side chapel of St Thomas of Canterbury, built, so they say, over a vault full of skeletons, which Nicholas secretly dreaded. The Almshouses are still there, and so is the bridge; and the old packhorse way along the crest of the hill, which you will notice in the heading of Chapter I, has become the motor road from Oxford to Cheltenham and Gloucester.

The Fetterlocks are an imaginary family, and there is no brass in Burford church to Nicholas's grandparents, but there are similar brasses to other wool-men, both here and in Northleach church, with merchants' marks on them resembling the one that I have invented.

Northleach, too, is a small town with a magnificent

church, bearing testimony to the riches of the local wool merchants. Master Midwinter lies buried there, and you can see his brass. He was a well-known wool-trader, and there are many references to him in the letters of that very Master Richard Cely, merchant of the Staple, who in real life rode round the Cotswolds with a hawk on his wrist buying wool.

The map at the beginning of the book shows the journeys Nicholas took with his father. They crossed the Thames at Radcot Bridge, and Master Fetterlock remarked that it had stood for two hundred years, and he wouldn't wonder if it stood for two hundred more. As that was in 1493, and the bridge is still there, he was quite right. The little statue has gone, but part of its pedestal remains. The picture of Radcot Bridge is on page 94.

At Newbury the church of St Nicholas was rebuilt about thirty years after the date of this story – Master Bradshaw remarked that it was far too small (page 111) and Jack o' Newbury, the most famous of the Newbury clothiers paid for the rebuilding. The central group in the picture of the Corpus Christi procession (on page 150) was actually suggested by a newspaper photograph of the Corpus Christi procession in Newbury in 1950 which I saw quite by chance while working on these pictures.

The George Inn at Winchester, several times rebuilt, still flourishes, and the Cathedral is, of course, in structure at least, very much as it was when Nicholas went there. Southampton is greatly changed, though there is enough of the old town left for you to be able to work out the reconstruction of it which appears at the beginning of Chapter 16. The Bargate was then strongly fortified with portcullis and drawbridge, as it was the landward entrance to the city. It stands now in the middle of the main road, with traffic passing on both sides of it; but you can go under the arched gateway into the little office of the Town Broker, where Master Fetterlock searched for records of his stolen wool. A great deal of the city walls, and traces of the moat which flowed outside them, remain. The moat with the sea turned Southampton into an island fortress. Probably in those days boats were towed round the moat to land goods at one or other of the small watergates. The drawing on page 185 is very tiny, but I hope it may give you an idea of what Nicholas saw as they rode towards the city in 1493. The Wool House (picture on page 188) remains, outwardly, almost unchanged.

Leap, near the mouth of the Beaulieu river, is now so tiny a hamlet that it is marked only on big maps, but the crossing from Leap to Gurnards Bay on the Isle of Wight was the route used normally by the Romans, who made a road through the New Forest from Leap to Southampton. It is also perfectly true that ships used to call on their outward voyages off the south-east coast of the Island to pick up supplies of the drinking water which stayed fresh longer than any other.

In Chapter 3 Messer Antonio explains to Nicholas the purpose of the bronze medal of Lorenzo de Medici, illustrated on page 40. You can see this actual medal in the Victoria and Albert Museum in London, and lots of others like it, both of famous people and of ordinary long-forgotten people too. These medals, in a sense the forerunners of the modern photograph, were the only means by which a man could have his portrait reproduced, so that he could give copies to his friends. If you go to the Museum, try to spend a little time at the big glass-topped cabinets with sliding drawers, where all these medals are beautifully arranged. You will find them fascinating – rather like peeping into a very old photograph album. But unlike photographs, these bronzes cannot fade. They look just the same today as they did when they were first made.

At the Victoria and Albert Museum you can also see the original of the stool on page 49, the spoon and fork on page 109, and jars very like the ones which Messer Antonio brought from Italy full of sweetmeats, as well as many other of the small objects pictured throughout the book.

Finally, you may care to know that the doings of the Lombard, Messer Antonio Bari, are founded on fact, though for the purposes of the story I have changed the name and date. There was, in 1458, a famous inquiry at the Guildhall about the offences of one Messer Simon Nori, a distinguished Lombard Merchant and agent of the Medici, who was accused of smuggling wool and of inducing the wool-packers to 'beard' the sacks.

Heard about the Puffin Club?

... it's a way of finding out more about Puffin books and authors, of winning prizes (in competitions), sharing jokes, a secret code, and perhaps seeing your name in print! When you join you get a copy of our magazine, *Puffin Post*, sent to you four times a year, a badge and a membership book.

For details of subscription and an application form, send a stamped addressed envelope to:

The Puffin Club Dept A
Penguin Books Limited
Bath Road
Harmondsworth
Middlesex UB7 ODA

and if you live in Australia, please write to

The Australian Puffin Club
Penguin Books Australia Limited
P.O. Box 257
Ringwood
Victoria 3134